mutation

The PHOENIX FILES

Chris Morphew

mutation

Kane Miller
A DIVISION OF EDC PUBLISHING

First American Edition 2012
Kane Miller, A Division of EDC Publishing

Text copyright © 2010 Chris Morphew
Illustration and design copyright © 2010 Hardie Grant Egmont
Design by Sandra Nobes
Typesetting by Ektavo

First published in Australia in 2010 by Hardie Grant Egmont

For information contact:
Kane Miller, A Division of EDC Publishing
P.O. Box 470663
Tulsa, OK 74147-0663
www.kanemiller.com
www.edcpub.com
www.usbornebooksandmore.com

Library of Congress Control Number: 2011935701

Printed and bound in the United States of America
4 5 6 7 8 9 10
ISBN: 978-1-61067-093-7

To the real-life Jordans and Georgias at PLC Sydney.
May you keep on living great stories!

Chapter 1

My fists clenched in my lap as Shackleton approached the podium, a hint of his sick, grandfatherly smile still pulling at his lips. He stared down at the coffin, clearing his throat with a sound like a dying animal.

I shivered, digging my nails down through the fabric of my skirt. *You already killed him, you filthy parasite. Isn't that enough?*

"Friends," Shackleton began solemnly, his arms casting long shadows out towards us. "Thank you all so much for being here. Officer Reeve was a dear friend of mine, and it is an honor and a privilege to be laying him to rest here this evening."

We were in a clearing in the bush at the northwest corner of town, where the Shackleton Co-operative had set up a makeshift cemetery. They hadn't thought to include one in the original designs for the town. Phoenix was the one place where people *weren't* supposed to die.

There were maybe fifty people at the funeral. Almost half were colleagues of Reeve's from the security center, neat rows of black uniforms melting together in the shadows of the trees.

Luke, Peter and I had debated all week whether it was even worth showing up, knowing Shackleton would be running the service, knowing it was only ever going to be an insult to Reeve's memory.

But here we were.

"Reeve was a great man," Shackleton said. "A loving husband, a devoted father, and a security officer of the highest caliber."

Luke leaned forward in the seat next to mine. He let out a heavy breath and put his head in his hands.

It had been a week since our disastrous trip to the Shackleton Building. A week since Shackleton had ordered Reeve's brutal execution right in front of us.

Two other men had died that night, but neither of them had been given a memorial service. If anyone asked, they'd been "dismissed due to professional misconduct."

But Reeve had family in Phoenix, so his death was harder to explain away. The Co-operative was forced to concoct an elaborate story about a malfunctioning ventilation unit and Reeve getting sliced up by one of the fans.

They'd done a pretty slick job of it too. Blood on the fan blades. Aaron Ketterley coming forward and corroborating the whole thing. All pretty grizzly, though nothing compared to the true horror of that night.

Almost without thinking, I reached behind and traced a finger over the weeping scab on the small of my back, the mark of my failed attempt to take a kitchen knife to Shackleton's tracking device. It was healing up surprisingly fast, given the mess I'd made.

But the suppressor was still there. A little piece of Shackleton buried in my skin, touching me, dirtying my insides. I didn't care what Luke said, I could *feel* it.

Shackleton paused to survey the crowd, and I drew my hand back to my lap.

"To his wife, Katie, and son, Lachlan," he continued, nodding at a seat in the front row, "I offer my deepest condolences. Know that the Shackleton Co-operative stands beside you in your grief."

Lachlan rocked back and forth on his mum's lap, oblivious to Shackleton's words. He was dressed in a little shirt and tie, tears running down his face. He stared around at the rest of us like he was expecting to find his dad waiting for him somewhere in the crowd.

I imagined Georgia sitting there in his place, all dressed up, trying to make sense of all these miserable grown-ups. I thought of Mum, in and out of the medical center all week, and I imagined what it would be like if anything happened to her, imagined trying to explain to my little sister why one of *our* parents was never –

Tears pricked my eyes, but I fought them back. No way was Shackleton going to see me lose it.

I caught Peter watching me. Probably trying to figure out if he could get away with putting his hand on my knee. I glared at him and he quickly turned his head the other way.

"If there is anything – *anything* – we can do to ease your suffering in this tragic time," said Shackleton, "please do not hesitate to let me know."

Reeve's wife gave a shaky nod.

I gritted my teeth, not knowing how much longer I could just sit here and absorb this. Shackleton tearing this family apart, murdering an innocent man like it was no worse than squashing a bug, and now standing up there getting weary, grateful smiles from the woman he'd made a widow.

Shackleton paused again, his gaze suddenly resting on Luke, Peter and me.

My skin crawled. Shackleton's smile stretched the tiniest bit wider.

"More than anything else, I will remember Officer Reeve as a man dedicated to protecting the town he loved, a man who treasured the values that we at the Shackleton Co-operative hold dear."

I shifted in my chair. I'd known all along that this night would be a travesty, but to use it to turn Reeve into a poster boy for all the evil being

5

committed in this place …

Luke grabbed hold of my arm, warning me to keep it together. I shook him off, but settled back down into my seat.

"My dear friends," Shackleton spread his arms wide again and lifted his voice, gearing up for his big finish. "What better way to honor the memory of this great man than by working together to ensure that Phoenix continues to be the place of safety, security and freedom that Officer Reeve fought so hard to –"

BOOM!

A second later, the old man was facedown on the ground. The sky flashed orange and the bushland behind him erupted into flame.

Chapter 2

The crowd was on their feet in a second, gasping and shouting and knocking over their seats.

"Crap," hissed Peter, craning his neck. "Now who's trying to kill us?"

Somewhere out in the bush, a fireball the size of a house had just blasted up above the tree line, impossibly bright against the darkening sky. I climbed up on top of my chair, staggering under the wave of blinding heat sweeping through the clearing. Even after all the rain we'd been getting, I could see flames starting to crawl up through the trees.

"What is it?" Luke looked up at me. "Can you see anything?"

I bit my lip, knowing right away what he was thinking.

Could this have something to do with his dad? Had he somehow escaped being hunted down by Shackleton's people? Had he convinced the outside world to come looking for us?

Were we being rescued?

Don't, I told myself, clamping down on my own wishful thinking. *Not now. Believe it when it happens.*

"Jordan?" Luke pressed.

"No," I said. "Nothing. Just fire."

I jumped back down to the ground and started pushing through the half-darkness for a closer look, past upturned chairs and forgotten handbags and wild speculation about terrorists and meteorites and plane crashes. Somewhere in all the confusion, little Lachlan was screaming his head off.

I sidestepped between another couple of people and suddenly I was right in front of Reeve's casket. I reeled back, startled by the sight of the still, dark form in the middle of all of this chaos, like for a minute I'd forgotten why we were here in the first place.

The guilt reared up again.

If we hadn't asked him to help us …

A figure appeared from behind the casket, and I jumped back. It was Shackleton, getting to his feet, looking as surprised as the rest of us, but also kind of excited.

"And there I was, worrying that my eulogy didn't have quite a punchy enough ending," he coughed, resting an arm on Reeve's casket. "Lovely to see you in three dimensions again, Ms. Burke. Not that I haven't been keeping an eye, of course," he tapped the side of his head, like I couldn't figure out what an eye was. "But that blinking dot on my computer monitor really does not do you justice."

I glared at him, and Shackleton's eyes glinted. He was insane, but not Crazy Bill insane. Shackleton knew exactly what he was doing. He paused for a moment to brush the dirt off his suit, then started calling out orders to the guards.

"Alonzo – get in there and find out what we're dealing with. Parker – would you be so kind as to track down Officer Calvin for me? I dare say he'll want to take a look at this. The rest of you – get these people back into town." Shackleton caught my eye and smiled again. "We wouldn't want anyone to get hurt now, would we?"

He drummed his fingers on the lid of the casket, clearly enjoying himself.

I was one breath away from taking a swing at him, but a glimpse of an approaching guard held me back. I'd seen this guy around town before. Officer Barnett, I think. He had an orange goatee and a face that said he'd have no problem getting violent if it came to that.

"All right, Ms. Burke," he said. "Let's get you home."

Barnett brought a hand down onto my shoulder. I might not have known him too well, but Calvin had made certain that his security team knew *exactly* who we were.

"Oi!" said Peter, as he and Luke burst out of the crowd. "Hands off!"

The guard smirked, tightening his grip on me. Peter glared, and I felt a surge of frustration. He always picked the dumbest moments to try to be a gentleman.

"Let's go," said Barnett, pushing me forward.

He marched us out of the clearing and back down the road into town, roping one of his friends in to help keep an eye on us.

I noticed none of the other funeral-goers were getting such special treatment.

"Don't think you can handle us all by yourself?" I muttered, wrenching free of him.

Officer Barnett just snarled.

By the time we got out of the bush, half the town had come out into the street to see what was going on. A woman with curly hair and a little girl in her arms came running up as we stepped out of the bush.

"Is everything all right?" she asked. Her eyes fell on Luke, Peter and me, and I bit my tongue, knowing what was coming. "Officer, what's going on out there? Did *those three* do something?"

Barnett shook his head. "Lightning strike."

"*Lightning* strike?"

"Back to your home please, ma'am," the guard said firmly. "We've got skid units coming through, and they're going to need –"

"YOUR ATTENTION PLEASE, LADIES AND

11

GENTLEMEN," another officer's voice boomed through a megaphone. "PLEASE CLEAR THE STREET IMMEDIATELY TO MAKE WAY FOR EMERGENCY FIRE CREWS."

The instructions got a few people moving, but others were still arriving. The explosion must have been heard all over town, and now there was a pillar of black smoke towering into the sky above the bush.

"Barnett! Cook!" shouted the officer with the megaphone. "We could use a hand over here if you're not too busy chatting!"

"Yeah, hang on!" Barnett called back, looking like he'd love to take that megaphone and smack the guy over the head with it. He barked at us, "Straight home. All of you."

The curly-haired woman shot one last dirty look at me and the boys, and then headed back across the street.

I turned, bristling, and led Luke and Peter off in the direction of my house, glancing back over my shoulder to keep an eye on Barnett. He watched until he was satisfied that we were actually leaving, then he and Cook ran off to help with the crowd.

"Freaking *moron,*" spat Peter.

"Which one?" asked Luke.

"All of them!" said Peter, not noticing that I was veering off the path. "This whole bloody town! If they had any idea of the crap we've been through trying to save their – Whoa! Jordan, no. Seriously. *No.*"

It was really getting dark now, and a flickering orange glow was shining out through the bushland to our left. The bushland I was heading straight back into.

"Come on," I said, "you don't want to know what's going on out –?"

"*Down!*" yelled Luke out of nowhere, grabbing Peter and me by the arms and dragging us into the dirt.

There was a flash of light and a roar of sound and at first I had no idea what was going on. After almost two months in Phoenix, there were some things my brain was just not used to dealing with anymore.

Headlights.

Engines.

A second later, three identical vehicles came

tearing down the narrow bike path towards us, gleaming black ATVs with red Shackleton Co-operative logos emblazoned on the sides. Each one had a single driver and a couple of other officers at the back, hanging off a little caged section packed with hoses and water tanks and other firefighting gear. The little ATVs looked like they'd been custom-designed with Phoenix in mind.

The first one flashed past our hiding place and I heard Peter swear.

Officer Calvin was crouched at the back, staring out at the fire like he was going to destroy it with his bare hands. No crutch. No bandages. No sign at all that he'd been smashed half to death only a few weeks ago.

I knew he'd been recovering quickly, but seriously – *no one* heals that fast.

The ATVs swerved through the crowd and raced up the dirt track towards the cemetery.

"See?" said Peter, getting up off the ground. "Another *excellent* reason not to go back out there."

He was probably right.

But clearly we couldn't just *not* investigate.

I got up and started bashing my way into the bush, knowing they wouldn't let me go out there alone.

"Jordan, no!" Peter hissed at me. "Wait! Let's just –"

He broke off into a sigh and a second later I heard footsteps crashing through the undergrowth.

"I swear, Jordan," Peter grumbled as the two of them caught up, "you get me killed tonight and I am going to haunt you *so freaking much.*"

I stumbled forward, almost tripping over a rock buried in the grass. The bush at the north end of town was a mess of dense trees and tall grass, and stomping through this way would be a lot slower than taking the cemetery path. But it would also give us more to hide behind as we got within eyeshot of security.

"What about the suppressors?" said Luke urgently. "Shackleton's going to know exactly where we –"

"Shackleton's too busy dealing with this to worry about what we're doing," I said, trying to ignore the dull throb at the base of my spine, the sudden rush of images of Dr. Montag holding me down over the table, digging that needle into me, Shackleton grinning down from the sidelines –

Stop it. You've got work to do.

The fire was maybe fifty meters away now, and I could feel the heat pressing against us. The flames lit up the bush, casting everything in hyperactive, flickering shadows.

"You guys didn't see anything before the explosion, did you?" asked Luke. "Like a plane, or –?"

"We would've *heard* a plane," said Peter. "What, you reckon this is someone's idea of a rescue plan? Bomb the trees and fly away again?"

I heard shouts up ahead, and engine noises. Calvin and his men had reached the explosion site. Pushing closer, I could make out the fire crews unreeling their hoses and aiming them into the flames. Loud hissing noises broke out over the crackling and snapping of the fire as the hoses began spewing water into the air.

I slowed down as we closed in on the explosion site. I held up a hand to stop the others, and we crouched down in the grass, searching for the best way forward.

The air around us was a haze of smoke and steam, glowing orange in the firelight. Calvin was standing in the middle of it all, shouting orders. He turned in our direction and I dropped further down into the grass.

"He's seen us!" Luke hissed.

"No, he hasn't," I said, watching his face, hoping I was right. "Quiet!"

Calvin turned around again. He got the attention of a couple of officers and pointed out across the grass to where we were hiding. I saw Luke's hands flash to the ground, ready to push off and run.

"No, *wait*," I said. "It's not us. He's telling them to concentrate on this end of the fire. Keep it away from the town." I started edging my way around to the right. "We're okay. We just need to get around to the other side before –"

Crack!

Luke shoved me to the ground, knocking me clear of the flaming branch that had just snapped off a tree above our heads. The branch crashed into the grass, sending a cloud of sparks shooting up into the air.

"Thanks," I breathed, scrambling back up again.

Peter rolled his eyes.

But now the grass around the branch was starting to curl and spark. Any second now, this whole area would be up in smoke.

"Here!" called one of the guards. "Quick!"

A burst of cold mist rained down across my face. Calvin's men were right on top of us.

I twisted around and started clawing away through the grass, forgetting all about being quiet, hoping the fire and the hoses and the shouting of the guards would be enough to disguise our escape.

I definitely hadn't dressed for the occasion. My shoes were slipping and my knees kept catching on the hem of my skirt. I stumbled again, almost crashing face-first into another rock, throwing down my hands just in time.

Hang on …

Squinting in the firelight, I saw that it wasn't a rock at all. It was a hunk of concrete, flat on one side and jagged on all the others, like it had broken off something much bigger.

Or exploded off.

"Hurry!" hissed Peter behind me, nudging my leg.

I pushed the concrete aside and kept moving.

This was ridiculous. We couldn't just crawl around in the grass all night. I glanced back over my shoulder to check on the guards, then ducked behind the nearest tree.

Luke and Peter got up after me, both looking like they'd much rather stay cowering in the grass. I waited until they were behind me again, then started circling around to the far side of the fire, keeping as low as I could, using the shadows to cover me.

The fire crews were slowly getting the blaze under control, extinguishing what was left of our light. I dashed along from tree to tree, eyes peeled for some sign of Shackleton. I finally spotted him, twenty meters away, at the top of a little rise, crouching in the dirt with his back to us. He had his head down, examining something.

I saw Calvin coming up to talk to him, jogging around in a wide arc like there was something on the ground out there that he was avoiding. Shackleton stood up as Calvin approached, and the two of them began talking.

"Need to get closer," I said, straining to hear.

"Too dangerous," said Luke. "We should go. Come back later when they've all cleared –"

"Wait here," I whispered.

"Jordan!"

But I was already out from behind my tree and creeping through what was left of the undergrowth. Up ahead, only a few meters behind Calvin and Shackleton, was the enormous blackened shell of another fallen tree, still smoldering at the edges. I dropped behind it.

"... report no unusual activity on the perimeter," Calvin was saying. "No air traffic, either."

"Come now, Bruce," said Shackleton lightly. "Do you really think that whatever did this came from the *air?*"

Calvin was silent for a moment. "Sir, that's – The ground was supposed to be stable!"

"Indeed," said Shackleton.

I held my breath, waiting for him to continue. But apparently that was all I was going to get.

I crouched there in the ash, listening to the crackle of the fire and the spraying of hoses.

It didn't take long for my patience to run out. I stretched up a couple of inches, risking a look over the top of the fallen tree.

Whoa.

A giant crater stretched out in front of

Shackleton's feet, big enough to fit my whole house inside. Security officers skirted around the outside, fighting back the flames.

In what was left of the light, I thought I could make out more hunks of concrete lodged into the sides of the massive hole. And there was something else too – a flickering light, different from the fire. Like something electrical, sparking.

Calvin shifted his weight and I ducked again.

"What do we tell people?" I heard Calvin say.

"Rope off the area," said Shackleton. "Tell them it was arson."

"Arson," said Calvin. "Committed by who?"

Shackleton chuckled. "Who do you think?"

Chapter 3

"Jordan! Jordan! Jordan! You have to get up! You –
have – to – get – *up!*"

"*Oof!*" I grunted as a heavy weight came crashing
down on top of me.

Two little hands grabbed my shoulders and a mess
of hair fell over my cheeks. I opened my eyes and saw
Georgia staring down at me, her face an inch from mine.

"Boo!" she shouted. She sat up on my stomach
and started giggling.

"Get off me," I mumbled, rolling over.

"Mum says you have to hurry up and get out
of –" Georgia's nose wrinkled. "Gross," she said,
jumping to the floor. "You smell!"

She ran out of the room, screaming down the hallway towards the kitchen. "Mum! How come Jordan stinks so much?"

I rolled out of bed and took my towel from the hook on the door.

I'd been stuck behind that fallen tree for about ten minutes last night, waiting until Calvin and Shackleton finally moved on to supervise the officers on the south side of the fire. We headed home after that, and I'd jumped straight into the shower before Mum or Dad had a chance to wonder why I was caked in ash and dirt. But apparently, that one quick wash hadn't been enough to get the smoke smell out of my skin.

I stopped on my way out of the shower and peered through the little bathroom window, into the bush below. I was desperate to get back out there, to get a good look at the crater, but I knew that would be a mistake. For now, at least. Shackleton would be back at work today, back to monitoring our every move from the computer in his office.

When I got down to the kitchen, Dad had already left for work and Mum was rushing around, trying

23

to sort out Georgia's breakfast and get herself ready at the same time. From the shadows under her eyes, I guessed she'd slept pretty badly last night. Again.

The toaster popped just as I walked through the door. Mum moved to get it.

"I'll do it," I said, wanting to make myself useful. Wanting to remind her that I wasn't a total delinquent.

"Thanks," said Mum, turning back to take a bite of her own breakfast.

Between the dramas with Mum's pregnancy and being completely cut off from our extended family, things had been pretty strained around here for a while. And hearing that their firstborn had been targeted as a security risk by the Shackleton Co-operative definitely hadn't improved Mum and Dad's moods.

Not that they wanted to believe that I was a thief and a vandal and whatever else the Co-operative was accusing me of – but at the same time, they couldn't really understand why someone would just make all of that up.

And I was refusing to defend myself. Not because

they wouldn't believe me. Because they *would*. Even if they hadn't put their finger on it yet, they could tell that things in Phoenix weren't adding up. Hearing that the Co-operative used me to cover up their mess would be all it took to push my parents over the edge.

And that terrified me more than anything.

I buttered Georgia's toast and then put a couple of slices in for myself. I kept telling myself that one day, when this was all over, when Shackleton and his flesh-eating genocide weapon were both taken care of, things would go back to normal again. Until then, I could deal with a few minor domestics if it meant keeping my family safe.

Five minutes later, I was out the door. I rode the long way around the block, not wanting to deal with Peter *accidentally* running into me on the way to school. Subtlety was not exactly a strong suit for that boy.

But he jumped between you and a loaded gun, I reminded myself. *That's not nothing.*

I rode towards the main street, skin crawling the way it always did when I passed the Shackleton

Building. After a month of trying, we'd done nothing to hit back against Shackleton. Nothing to even slow him down. Every attempt just ended in more blood and nightmares, and that was *before* he realized what we were up to. Before the threats to our families. Before the suppressors.

I didn't even have my *body* to myself anymore.

I knew it wouldn't be long before the "news" broke about our involvement with the fire. The Shackleton Co-operative would have an article ready for this afternoon's edition of the *Phoenix Herald*.

It'd probably be Peter's dad's job to write it up. I imagined him sitting there in his office, in that wheelchair they'd put him in, forced to keep poisoning the whole town against his own son. By the end of the day, they'd have *arson* to add to our list of imaginary –

A wave of nausea flooded up out of nowhere.

I stumbled off my bike and doubled over, cringing, knowing what was coming, holding my head in both hands as though that was somehow going to stop it.

Please. Not again. Not n –

Everything shifted.

The sky turned black.

Rain splashed down.

The streetlights flickered on, casting glowing circles onto the wet ground.

And everyone else in the town center flashed out of existence. Vanished.

But I wasn't alone. Luke and Peter were suddenly right there with me, and –

"*It's the baby,*" Dad shouted. "*There's something wrong with the baby!*"

He was supporting Mum with one arm, cradling a hysterical Georgia in the other. Dr. Montag was crouched over Mum, hands on her stomach. Everything was jerky and blurred, like I was watching it all on a handheld video camera being operated by a five-year-old. The rain spattered down around me, but somehow it never touched my skin.

Backwards, I thought. *I've gone backwards this time.*

I'd been here before. A week ago, right after we left the Shackleton Building.

"*We have to get her to the medical center,*" said

27

Montag as Mum groaned again.

"No!" shouted a familiar voice.

My voice.

The world went even blurrier for a second, and suddenly it was like there were two of me. Another Jordan stepped forward, out of the place where I was standing. She stumbled towards Montag, exactly like I'd done a week ago, legs only barely keeping her upright. It couldn't have been more than fifteen minutes since he'd injected her with the suppressor.

No one else batted an eyelid as the two of us moved apart from each other.

It's all in your head, I told myself. *A memory. You're not really here.*

But it was more than that. My memory couldn't turn day into night, couldn't call rain down out of nowhere, couldn't zap my mind out of the present against my will.

Not before Phoenix, anyway.

"Get your hands off her!" shouted the me from back then.

Dad shot her a bewildered look. Why in the world wouldn't I want them to go to the medical center?

"Mrs. Burke," said Montag, straightening up and throwing a hand out across the street. *"Please, we need to get moving."*

His sleeve pulled away from his arm a bit, and I noticed a mark on his wrist that I hadn't seen the first time around. A number, scribbled in blue pen: *1308.*

Before I had time to wonder about it, Dad turned in my direction, thrusting Georgia into the other Jordan's arms. The other Jordan staggered, the pain from the suppressor jolting through her legs, but managed to stay standing. Concern rose in Dad's face, but then Mum cried out again. Dad hoisted her up into the air and took off across the street with the doc.

The other Jordan tried to follow – but she couldn't do it. It had taken Peter's dad days to even walk in a straight line after his injection. No way was week-ago me about to go sprinting across town. She swayed on her feet, gritting her teeth in frustration, and I stiffened, knowing the agony she was going through.

Dad glanced back over his shoulder, probably wondering why we weren't coming after them. But then Montag called to him again and he kept running.

Peter put an arm around the other Jordan, trying to help. But he was even worse on his feet than she was. The other Jordan shrugged him off and he almost fell over backwards. She muttered an apology and started patting Georgia on the back, telling her it was all going to be okay.

Mum let out a scream. I glanced back and forth between her and the other Jordan, feeling the panic and the fear and the helplessness all over again. And then it finally dawned on me.

Week-ago Jordan couldn't go chasing after Mum and Dad. But maybe I could.

I broke into a run, bolting away across the wet concrete.

As soon as I started moving, the world blurred out of focus again.

Dad and Montag were already halfway up the medical center steps. I surged ahead, only just keeping my balance. The whole street rippled and smeared around me. It was like running on a waterbed. Then the nausea welled up again. I lost my footing and slammed to the ground on my hands and knees.

Georgia broke off, mid-scream.

The sun flashed on.

The rain disappeared.

The street was crowded with people again.

I was back. Back in the present. Back in the real world.

I squeezed my eyes shut, dazed, gagging, but fighting it down. I could feel the beginnings of a headache creeping up from the base of my skull, but it didn't seem like it would be as bad as the last couple. That was something, at least.

"Are you all right?" asked a concerned voice from somewhere above me.

"Careful," said someone else, a man this time. "It's the Burke girl."

I stared up at the two of them. Suits and newspapers and coffee cups. Other people had stopped too, looking on from a distance. Just *waiting* for me to do something crazy and give them all a story to tell when they got into work. I blocked them out, pulling my bike upright again. A couple of security officers were coming over to investigate, and I really didn't feel like explaining my fainting spell to them.

31

I rode away in the other direction, thinking that I'd had enough enemies in this place already before my own brain started turning against me.

I found Luke and Peter loitering at the lockers. They both looked kind of uneasy, like they'd just been arguing. Which probably meant that it had something to do with me.

"Hey, what happened to you?" asked Luke, eyeing the grazes on my hands and knees.

"Nothing," I nudged him aside to get to my locker. "Just stacked it on the way here."

"You okay?" asked Peter.

"I'm fine," I said, snatching up my science book with both hands before he could get a good look at them. "Any news on last night?"

"Not yet," said Peter. "I mean, people are talking, but it's all crap. No one knows anything. And they're not asking us about it, so Shackleton's cover story obviously hasn't gotten out yet."

"Pryor?" I asked.

Luke shook his head. There'd been no sign of her

all last week. And after the debacle in the Shackleton Building where we'd used *her phone* to contact Luke's dad, we thought it was pretty safe to assume our staff-student liaison officer jobs had been canned.

"Good," I said.

We started back up the corridor, weaving through the morning rush.

"Hey, Jordan," Luke began, in a voice that was trying a bit too hard to be offhand. I saw Peter's expression shift, and I had a feeling I was about to discover what they'd been arguing over.

"Mm?" I said.

Luke hesitated for just a second. "You doing anything tomorrow night?" he asked.

"Huh?" I said, caught off guard. "No, I don't think so. Why?"

"Mum's having Montag over for dinner. I thought maybe you'd like to come. You know, to see if we can get anything out of him."

"Oh," I said. "Yeah, sure, of course."

"He asked me too," said Peter quickly. "Can't come, though. Got a family thing."

I raised an eyebrow. "Um, okay."

"No! Please!" gasped a high-pitched voice from around the corner. "I didn't mean it! I didn't mean it!"

"Should've thought of that before you did it," said a deeper voice.

"Tank," said Peter, pushing through the crowd.

I groaned. *Now what?*

We rounded the corner just in time to see Tank's enormous fist go slamming down into the mouth of a tiny, pale-skinned Year 7 kid. It was Jeremy, the kid they all called Ghost.

"Stop!" he begged, cowering on the ground. "Please – I didn't do anything!"

"Shut up," said Tank, throwing a fist at Jeremy's gut.

A dark-haired guy stood a few steps away, next to a girl wearing half her body weight in makeup. Mike and Cathryn, Tank's friends. Both looking stony-faced and not at all surprised.

This wasn't just some random outburst. They were all in on it.

Jeremy was being *punished*.

Whump!

The next blow caught him square in the chest.

I saw Luke cringe. He knew exactly what this kid was going through. Jeremy was starting to cry now. He tried to scramble away, but there was a reason why his attacker was called Tank.

I'd seen enough. "Oi!" I shouted, storming over. "Get off him!"

Tank kept right on punching.

"Stay out of this, Jordan," said Mike, glaring at me from behind his sunglasses. He moved between me and the beating. "Not your fight."

"It is now," I muttered, shoving past and gripping Tank's shoulders with both hands. I pulled him back hard. He took a couple of stumbling steps backwards, and then twisted around, trying to claw me off.

"Let go of me, you dumb b –"

"*WHAT* DO YOU TWO THINK YOU ARE DOING?"

Mr. Hanger had just come roaring in from the quad. I dropped from Tank's shoulders and turned to face him.

Tank glanced over at Mike, looking for instructions. Mike shook his head.

"Sir!" said Peter. "Tank was beating up one of the

Year 7s! Jordan was just trying to –"

"Quiet, Peter," Mr. Hanger snapped.

Jeremy was still crying on the floor. I reached out a hand and pulled him up.

Mr. Hanger strode closer to the two of us. "Anything you'd like to tell me, Jeremy?"

Jeremy opened his mouth to explain, but then Tank held a fist up behind Mr. Hanger's back and he said, "No, sir."

"All right then," said Mr. Hanger. "All of you – *out*."

"Sir," I said, "you can't just –"

"You heard me, Miss Burke."

I glared at him, but gave up the argument. Couldn't risk getting Pryor involved.

Satisfied, Mr. Hanger walked off. I looked around for Jeremy, but he'd already made his escape.

Mike, Cathryn and Tank were halfway down the hall, heading out to the quad.

"So this is what you guys are doing for fun these days, huh?" Peter called after them. "Beating up little kids?"

"Only the ones who deserve it," said Mike.

Peter started after them, but I grabbed his arm. "Don't. Not now."

"Yeah," said Luke. "Bell's about to go anyway. We can corner them in science."

"Whoa – what's that?" said Peter. His attention had shifted to my hand around his arm.

I let go. "I already told you, I fell off my bike on the way."

"No, Jordan," said Luke. *"Look."*

I stared down at my right hand, the hand I'd used to help Jeremy up off the floor. It was covered in a patch of something pinkish-white.

No, not covered. *Stained.*

A whole patch of my skin had suddenly changed color from brown to white.

A patch of skin the exact size and shape of Jeremy's hand.

Chapter 4

"It still won't come off," I said, stretching out my hand to reveal the five-fingered birthmark wrapping around my palm and up my wrist, like Jeremy had dipped his hand in paint before grabbing me with it. I'd had a go at covering over the mark with some of Mum's concealer, but it was still pretty visible if you were looking for it.

When we'd gotten to science yesterday morning, I'd noticed that Tank's knuckles were the same – pale white in the places where they'd collided with Jeremy. The change wasn't as noticeable on Tank's lighter skin, but it was definitely still there.

Jeremy had stayed well clear of us all for the rest of the day.

Now it was late the next afternoon and I was over at Luke's place, waiting for Montag to arrive. It was weird being here without Peter. It shouldn't have been a big deal, but for some reason it left me feeling slightly on edge.

In my house, this upstairs bedroom belonged to Georgia. It was kind of unsettling to see it all scattered with inside-out clothes and video game magazines and smelling like boy. Since I'd been up here last, Luke had stuck a couple of old photos of him and his dad to the wall above his bed.

The doc was running late. If he didn't hurry up, Dad would be coming over to get me before we'd even had time to eat.

"Did your parents notice?" asked Luke, studying my hand.

"Nope," I said. "You know how distracted they both are lately. Besides, last night they were much more interested in having a 'discussion' about why I've suddenly turned into a pyromaniac."

"Bet that was fun," said Luke.

"They *know*," I said, before I'd even realized I was saying it. "They know I'm hiding something. Dad kept asking me these leading questions, like he *wanted* me to deny it all – and I almost …"

I sighed and sat down on the edge of Luke's bed. "Look, I know we can't tell them anything, but – They're just so *confused*. And it's hurting them. I can't keep this up forever. I don't know how much longer I can keep on pretending everything's all right."

Luke sat down next to me. "What is it now? Sixty-two days?"

"Sixty-one," I said.

"Right."

I stared out the window.

"Doesn't even make sense," said Luke eventually, breaking the silence. "They print these accusations, but then they don't even do anything about them. Not that it matters to my mum. She's still buying everything the Co-operative tells her – especially the stuff about me. But she's decided it's my way of coping with the divorce, and her thing with Montag, so she's being extra nice to me all of a sudden. Just waiting for me to get it out of my system and go back

40

to being a good little boy again." He rolled his eyes.

Luke was like the complete opposite of Peter.

Peter was erratic, all-over-the-place. You could put him in the same situation ten times and he'd react ten different ways.

Luke was much more straightforward. Not in a simple, predictable way. But I knew I could count on him to make sense.

He reached down and picked up my right hand, pulling me back to the present. But he wasn't looking at the handprint. He was looking at the graze I'd given myself yesterday morning.

"It happened again, didn't it?" he said. "Another one of your ... vision things."

"What makes you say that?" I said.

Luke gave me a look. "Since when do you just randomly fall off your bike on the way to school?"

He ran a finger across the graze on my palm, then suddenly seemed to realize what he was doing and dropped my hand back into my lap.

"Yeah," I said, losing focus for a second. "Yeah, you're right."

I stood up.

"What happened?" he asked.

"It was the night at the Shackleton Building. When all of the stuff with Mum's baby started. And it was the clearest one so far. The one of – of Reeve at Flameburger, and the one of the trapdoor thing in Pryor's office … They were just kind of *flashes*. You know, bits and pieces. But this one – I was there for, like, a good thirty seconds. A minute, even."

Luke got to his feet too. I expected him to come out with something sympathetic or reassuring, but instead he said, "Do you think they're connected?"

"What?"

"Your – Your visions or whatever they are, and Ghost's skin thing. Both happening here in Phoenix. I mean, it can't just be a coincidence, can it?"

My stomach turned. The same idea had occurred to me, but I'd been trying not to think about it. Because if me and Jeremy were both being affected by the same thing …

"Crap," said Luke, catching up. "Crazy Bill."

"Yeah," I said heavily. "Remember back in Ketterley's office? Ketterley and Calvin were talking about him. Ketterley was worried that whatever's happened to Bill might start happening to … other people. What if he was right? I mean, what if *that's* why Bill knows so much? Because he's seen it all already. What if I'm –?"

"Jordan, stop. You're not turning into Bill."

"You don't *know* what I'm –"

"We can fix it," he said firmly. "That's why we're fighting. So we can *stop* whatever's going on out here." He yanked my hand up in front of me. "Including this."

I stared at the hand for a second, then pulled it out of his grip.

"Yeah," I said. "You're right. Sorry."

"No, listen, you're not the only one who's –"

He broke off as the doorbell rang. "Montag," he said, warmth disappearing from his voice. "About time. You ready?"

We headed downstairs and found Luke's mum showing Montag into the dining room. When I'd arrived, she'd still had a suit on from her day in the office, but she'd obviously dressed herself up a bit in the meantime. Luke's eyes went dark at the sight of the skirt she was wearing.

Montag was standing with his back to us. Luke's mum looked past him and saw us coming through the doorway.

"Have a seat, guys!" she said, slipping into the kitchen. "Just getting the salad."

The doc turned around, and I almost smiled at the shocked expression on his face.

He didn't know we were coming.

"Luke," he said, recovering quickly as Ms. Hunter returned. "Good to see you again."

"Thought it was about time you two started getting to know each other a bit better," she smiled, putting the salad bowl down on the table.

"Ah, of course," said Montag. He pulled out a chair. "This looks wonderful, Emily."

The table was piled high with food: a big lamb roast (which made me wonder again where all our meat was coming from in this place), potatoes, salad and veggies, hot rolls …

Luke sat down at the table, fuming. He was always complaining that his mum never made the effort to cook anything, but it looked like she'd made an exception for the doc.

"Oh, it's not much, really," said Luke's mum, taking my plate and piling on a bit of everything. "How was work?"

"Same as usual," said Montag. "Run off my feet."

My chest tightened. Mum had been back at the medical center today for yet another appointment.

"And you?" the doc asked.

"Exhausting," Ms. Hunter sighed. "I barely got through anything with all the people coming in and out of my office. I assume you've heard about Luke's latest escapade?" She sent a disapproving look in my direction. Apparently, her tolerance for Luke's actions didn't extend to me.

Luke glared at his mum across the table. Even in a normal dinner situation, bringing your son's behavior issues up in front of your new boyfriend wasn't exactly a diplomatic move.

"I did read something about it in yesterday's paper," said Montag, buttering a roll. He looked up at Luke and me. "You children should be more careful. Keep carrying on like that and you're going to find yourself in some serious trouble."

I stabbed my fork down into a hunk of meat,

imagining it was Montag's leg.

"Funny how we managed to be in two places at once that night," I said. "Somehow getting that fire started even though we were sitting at Reeve's funeral the whole time. Pretty impressive, when you think about it."

Luke's mum pursed her lips.

Montag swallowed a mouthful of food and dabbed his beard with a napkin. "May I give you some advice, Jordan? If you ask me, you'd be far better off simply owning up to your indiscretions. Denial will only get you deeper into trouble."

"Yeah, thanks for the tip," I said coldly.

Luke's eyes twitched between me and the doc, and I could tell he was starting to wonder whether bringing me here had been such a good idea.

"Terrible what happened to that poor security officer," said Luke's mum abruptly. But if she was looking for a way to defuse the tension, she'd picked the wrong topic.

"Yeah," I said, staring at Montag. "Terrible."

"Quite tragic," he agreed, putting down his knife and fork for a moment. "Though his own recklessness played no small part in it."

My insides twisted again.

"Mm," said Luke's mum, taking a drink of water. "Trying to help out with some repairs or something, wasn't he?"

"Foolish," said Montag. "He was toying with things far beyond his understanding. He should have kept out of it."

"So Reeve deserved what he got, did he?" I said, raising my voice more than I'd meant to.

Ms. Hunter's face was beginning to turn red.

"It was an abject mess of a situation caused by reckless and irresponsible behavior," said Montag, gripping the table with both hands. "I did everything I could to save as many lives as possible."

"Well, you did a pretty crap job of it," Luke muttered.

"Luke!" his mum snapped.

"No, Emily, it's all right," said Montag in a tone that was completely at odds with the words coming out of his mouth. "It's natural for him to be angry. It's part of the grieving process."

Ms. Hunter narrowed her eyes at Luke, probably

wanting to know why on earth he needed to *grieve* the death of a man he barely knew. But before she had time to respond, the doorbell rang again.

I looked at my watch. Eight o'clock already. That would be Dad at the door.

Stupid curfew.

Ms. Hunter stood up. Tonight was really not going well for her.

Montag waited until she was out of the room. Then he leaned across the table, jabbing a finger at Luke and me.

"You foolish – arrogant – *children*," he hissed. "What could you *possibly* think you're achieving here?"

"So, what," I said, "you expect us to just lie down and take it?"

"Do you honestly believe you can stop what's being done here?" Montag said. "Like it or not, Jordan, the world has changed. This is the way things are now. The only question left to you is how much more blood you want on your hands before you accept that."

Things would've gotten ugly very quickly if Dad

hadn't walked into the room at that moment. He glanced at the doc, surprised to see him here, then down at me. I tried to wipe the anger from my face, but he must have caught the edge of it. "Jordan? You okay?"

"Yeah," I said, abandoning my half-finished meal. "C'mon. Let's go. Thanks for dinner, Ms. Hunter."

"Don't mention it," said Luke's mum tonelessly.

"Oh, Abraham, before you go …" The doc got up and crossed to talk to Dad. "Would it be possible for you and Samara to drop in to see me tomorrow?"

A little shiver sparked up my spine.

"Sure, doc," said Dad. "Have you figured out what's –?"

"I think it would be best if you waited and let me explain in the morning," Montag cut in. "I believe I've ascertained what's been troubling your wife and the baby …"

"But?" said Dad.

The doc looked uncomfortable. "Let's just say things may be slightly more complicated than we'd first thought."

Chapter 5

"Okay," said Georgia, gesturing excitedly with her hands as we walked down the street, "this time *you* can be the princess and I can be the dinosaur."

I glanced down at her. "Georgia, I don't think I really understand this game."

We reached the end of our block and I turned the corner, into another identical street lined with more identical houses. Prison cells dressed up as homes. Georgia stomped around behind me, arms up above her head like claws.

"Princess! Princess! I'm going to eat you up!"

Usually, I would have played along, but I just didn't have the head space for it today.

Mum and Dad were already on their way to see Dr. Montag. After a solid hour of pestering last night, they'd finally agreed to let me come with them – but first, I had to drop Georgia off at a friend's place.

Back home, there would have been a dozen aunts, uncles and grandparents falling over themselves to take Georgia for the day. Phoenix was a different story. It had taken Mum ages to find someone to mind her on such short notice.

I stopped at the house.

A second later, Georgia's hands clamped down on my hips.

"CHOMP! CHOMP! CHOMP!" she shouted, hammering me with her fingertips. "EAT! EAT! EAT!"

"Oi, *stop*," I said, batting her away with one hand and pulling the front gate open with the other. "Settle down, will you? We're here."

"I *know* we are!" said Georgia, letting go of me and rolling her eyes. She raced up the front walkway and started banging on the front door. I caught up to her just as the door swung open.

A freckle-faced girl stood in the doorway. It was Lauren, one of the Year 7s who'd pestered us almost nonstop during our stint as Pryor's staff-student liaisons.

For a second, I thought we'd come to the wrong house. But then I heard footsteps thundering up the hall behind her, and Georgia's friend Max poked his head out.

"Georgia!" he said. "I'm making a spaceship for us to live in!"

Georgia burst out laughing, and the two of them disappeared into the house.

"All right," I said, wanting to get down to the medical center ASAP. "Well, tell your mum –"

"Thank you for saving Jeremy," Lauren said in a rush.

"Huh?" I said. "Oh, right. No problem."

"No, seriously," said Lauren. "Thanks. If you hadn't come in, Tank would've …"

"What were they attacking him for anyway?" I asked.

"It was so stupid!" Lauren threw up her hands, like she'd been waiting for a chance to vent all of this. "Jeremy was just drawing on his school bag, and that other guy, Mike or whatever, saw what he was doing and just *lost* it."

"What was it?" I asked. "What was he drawing?"

She made a face, as though this was a weird question for me to be asking. "It was nothing!" she said. "Just this circle with – Hang on."

Lauren leaned inside, reaching for the phone table, and came back with a notepad and pen. She flipped to a blank page and started scribbling something.

"Here," she said, holding the notepad up in front of my face. "It was this."

She'd drawn a kind of spiral thing – a circle with a bunch of lines twisting out from the middle.

"What is it?" I asked.

"How should I know?" said Lauren. "I thought he just made it up, but obviously it meant something to Tank, because five seconds later he was smashing him onto the floor."

"Uh-huh," I said, but my attention had suddenly shifted away from the notepad, to the hand that was holding it. Between each of Lauren's fingers was a thick smudge of slightly paler, freckle-less skin.

She'd been holding hands with Jeremy.

Lauren caught me looking at her and whipped her hand around behind her back. "Anyway, thanks again," she said hurriedly. "Mum said she'd drop Georgia back at –"

But she was drowned out mid-sentence by a high-pitched squeal from down the hall. Georgia came bursting through the doorway, squeezing past Lauren's leg to get out of the house. Max was right behind her, swinging a little foam sword above his head. Georgia turned left and right, searching wildly for an escape route, then jumped up and started climbing me like a tree. Max ran circles around us, swatting the sword at Georgia's ankles.

"Help me!" she gasped between hysterical giggles. "Help me! He's gonna *kill* me!"

I reached down and snatched Max's sword out of his hand.

"Hey! That's *mine!*"

Lauren raised an eyebrow at me.

I looked at the sword, then shook my head and handed it back. "You be nice to my sister, okay?"

"I *am* being nice," Max said. "You're the one who's being a stealer!"

"Right," I said. "Sorry."

It had been a stupid overreaction. But I was starting to feel like that was the only way I knew how to deal with anything anymore. This place was messing with my head. And having Georgia here in the middle of it all was like this constant *weight*.

I had to protect her.

But how was I supposed to do that when I couldn't even keep my own brain under control?

Georgia was staring up at me, brow furrowed.

"What's wrong?" she asked.

"Nothing. Everything's fine."

Sixty days, I told myself. *Hang in there. Concentrate on the job in front of you. Concentrate on dealing with Tabitha —*

Georgia's eyes went wide. She grabbed me by the shirt, shivering like she'd just stepped into a freezer.

"Jordan," she whispered. "Who's Tabitha?"

I walked up the steps to the medical center, Georgia's terrified expression still burned into my mind.

Tabitha.

Had I accidentally said the name out loud?

Couldn't have, I thought. *No one else reacted. Just Georgia.*

And it wasn't just the name either. She was *afraid.* Like she knew Tabitha was something dangerous.

I stopped at the top of the steps, and turned instinctively to look back out at the town. Checking that the coast was clear, though I wasn't even up to anything. My eyes passed over the Shackleton Building. I imagined Shackleton sitting up there in his office, tracking my every move, and my lower back gave another dull throb.

The doors slid open to let me into the medical center. Mum and Dad were standing in the middle of the waiting room, talking to Dr. Montag.

The doc tensed up as I approached.

"Jordan wanted to sit in with us this morning," said Mum, apparently mistaking his frustration for confusion.

"That's not a problem, is it, doc?" I smiled.

"Of course not," said Montag, tightening his grip on the laptop under his arm. He looked back to Mum and Dad. "Shall we?"

I started towards Montag's office, then hesitated as the doc moved off in a different direction.

"This way, please."

The doc led us across to the other side of the reception area, down a winding corridor, to a door marked *STAFF ONLY.* He pulled out a key and let us in. We headed down a flight of stairs, along another corridor, and finally stopped at a tiny room with nothing in it but a desk and a few plastic chairs.

"I really must apologize," said Montag as he ushered us inside. "Maintenance are doing some work on my office today. Why they couldn't have chosen a more convenient time is beyond me, but ... Anyway. Please, have a seat."

He was lying.

Why? What was his *real* reason for dragging us all the way down here? What was he about to do to us that he didn't want anyone else to see?

"What have you got for us, doc?" asked Dad, the chair creaking under him as he sat down. He reached across and squeezed Mum's hand.

Montag took a breath. "All right," he said, setting his laptop down on the desk in front of us. "As you will recall, Samara, this all began just over a month ago when you first came in to see me, complaining of, among other things, intermittent nausea and shooting pains in your stomach. We ran a series of tests at the end of which I informed you that you were five weeks pregnant."

"Doc, we already know all this," Dad cut in. "Why are you –?"

"Because," said Montag delicately, "that assessment may not have been entirely accurate."

Silence.

Montag waited, face all doctorly calm.

"What are you saying?" asked Mum.

Montag turned to his computer and brought up an image of a little blob. Leaning forward, I could make out the shapes of a head and some tiny hands and feet.

"This is an average fetus at nine weeks," said Montag. "The image is at actual size – something approaching two centimeters. Based on my original assessment of your pregnancy, we would expect your baby to be at approximately this stage of development by now."

"But …?" said Mum.

"*But,*" Montag continued, "when I performed an ultrasound earlier this week, what I actually found was *this.*"

The doc clicked to the next image.

I jolted in my chair. Mum tightened her grip on Dad's hand.

The image in front of us had just exploded in size. We were now looking at a baby almost a quarter as big as the laptop screen.

Dad's face went cold. "I don't understand."

"Neither do I," said Montag. "At the moment, all I can tell you is what I've observed: as of a few days ago, your baby is just over fourteen centimeters in length and weighs in at approximately one hundred grams – figures more consistent with a baby at fifteen weeks."

"You're telling me I'm *fifteen* weeks pregnant?" said Mum. "Surely that should have been –"

"No," said Montag. "You're not. And you're not nine weeks pregnant either."

"But you told me –"

"Samara, my estimates were based on *normal* rates

59

of prenatal growth. But that's not what's happening here. Your baby is developing at remarkable speed. Somewhere between two and three times as fast as a normal pregnancy. You may actually have been carrying this child for as few as six weeks."

"Six weeks …" Mum repeated.

Which means she didn't get pregnant until after we got here, I realized.

"You're serious," said Dad, shaking his head at the doc. "You're actually – *How?* How is this happening?"

"I'm doing all I can to find out," said Montag. "But this situation is completely unprecedented."

The room went quiet again.

Mum's hands moved to her stomach, like she was trying to shield the baby from what the doc was telling her. Or maybe she was just searching for something solid and real in the middle of all of this insanity.

"What now?" said Dad eventually.

"Well," said Montag, "based on the current rate of growth, I'd say you've got no more than nine weeks before your baby reaches full term, which would put your due date somewhere in the vicinity of –" He broke off, eyes flickering in my direction for just a fraction of a second, "– somewhere in the vicinity of August 13."

Mum and Dad just nodded, completely missing the weight of what Montag had just said.

August 13.

Day Zero.

This baby was going to arrive just in time for the end of the world.

Chapter 6

I found Luke on the way into school the next day and filled him in on my impossible weekend. He listened to the whole thing without interrupting, although that may have been because he was too weirded out to speak.

After ten minutes of talking, I looked up to find myself standing at the bike racks outside the front office. I'd hardly even noticed where I'd been walking. We chained up our bikes and wandered out to the quad.

Luke leaned back against the wall of the industrial arts building. "Jordan, this is … insane. If you told all this to Peter, he'd say you were –"

"Yeah," I said. "That's why I'm talking to you about it."

Luke pursed his lips and my heart sank. If he didn't buy it either …

"Not that I don't believe you," he said quickly, catching the look on my face. "I mean, after everything else that's happened here … But this is –"

"Ridiculous," I finished. "Even for us. Yeah. I know."

Luke craned his neck, staring out behind me.

"What are you doing?" I asked.

"Nothing. I just – If Peter sees us hanging out like this …"

I rolled my eyes, sick of tiptoeing around Peter's stupid suspicions. "Let him see," I said. "It's not like we're even doing anything."

"Yeah, I know. I just don't want him to –"

"Don't want me to *what?*" snapped a voice from around the corner.

Luke flinched, face turning red.

Peter wheeled around the side of the building. I got the feeling he'd been waiting back there for a while now, choosing his moment to strike.

"Nothing," said Luke again. "I didn't mean –"

63

"No, come on mate," said Peter, storming over. "Tell me. What's gonna happen if I see you guys together? Huh? What am I going to do?"

"Well, I was going to say react badly," said Luke, recovering himself a bit, "but since you're being so calm about it all, I guess I was –"

He broke off as Peter took hold of his shirt.

"Oi!" I said. "Pete, c'mon."

But I doubt he even heard me.

"You reckon I don't get what's going on here?" he spat, looking slightly crazy now. "All this stupid freaking *don't-tell-Peter* crap?"

Luke sighed. "Peter –"

"No, you shut up and listen!" said Peter, shaking him. "This is my fight too, and I'm bloody sick of –!"

"ENOUGH!" I shouted, grabbing each of them before things could get any more out of hand.

Peter let go of Luke's shirt, shoving him back against the wall.

"You think this is helping?" I hissed, lowering my voice so I wouldn't be overheard by the kids who were stopping to watch us. "Three people against this whole town, and you want to start fighting *each other?*"

No response from either of them. Not that Luke had anything to answer for, but right now taking sides was only going to wind Peter up even more.

It wasn't the first time he'd blown up like this. We'd all lost it at some point. Hardly surprising, given everything we were going through.

But there was something different in Peter's anger. Something out of control. And it seemed to be taking less and less to set him off.

I let go of them both.

Peter blinked, like even he was surprised at the force of his outburst. "Sorry," he said, finally. But he was looking at me, not Luke.

"I need something out of my locker," I said, taking off towards the English building.

The others followed. Peter sped up to walk next to me, and I noticed a smudge of brown on his collar. I looked down at my hand. Some of the concealer had smeared off on his shirt when I'd grabbed him.

"We should track Jeremy down," I said. "See if –"

"Shh!" said Peter, putting his arm out to stop me. He'd stepped halfway around the corner, then darted back.

"What?"

But then I heard them. Hushed voices in the next corridor. Voices I recognized.

"What's the time?" asked Cathryn, sounding anxious.

"Twenty-one past," said Tank.

"Check it again."

"We just did," said Mike. "It's empty."

"Check it again," said Cathryn. "They said it was important."

"You think I don't know that?" said Mike.

"Both of you, shut up," Tank hissed. "Someone's going to hear us."

Mike sighed. He waited another few seconds.

"All right," he said. "Go on. Check it."

There was a clank of metal. I risked a look around the corner and saw the three of them crowded in front of an open locker about halfway down the hall.

"There!" said Tank.

Mike's hand shot into the locker and pulled out a yellowing envelope, sealed with black wax that matched his fingernails.

I flinched as someone gripped my shoulder. Peter,

66

leaning past me to see down the corridor.

"That's the locker!" he whispered as Mike ripped the envelope open. "The one we caught Cat going through."

"Get back," I said. "They'll see you."

"Yep," said Peter. "Reckon you might be right."

And then he was taking off down the corridor towards them.

Cathryn saw him coming and clutched Mike's shirt sleeve, color draining from her face.

Great, I thought, following Peter around the corner. *And you say I'm the reckless one.*

Mike looked up from the letter in his hand. Without missing a beat, he slipped it back into its envelope, stuck it in his pocket and said, "Hey, Pete. What's up?"

"What've you got there?" Peter asked, gesturing at Mike's pocket.

Mike's head turned towards Luke and me. "It's personal," he said.

"Yeah," said Peter, "I bet it is."

He lunged forward, knocking Mike back into the open locker and making a grab for the envelope.

"Hey – Weir – c'mon –" Mike grunted, shoving a

hand up into Peter's face. Peter turned his head, teeth clenched, still grasping for Mike's pocket. "Tank! You want to do something about this?"

Tank reached out and tore Peter off Mike.

"Oi! Let go!" Peter kicked and shook, but he didn't have a chance. Tank was easily twice as big as him.

Peter had left Mike half-sitting in the locker. His shirt pocket was hanging by a thread. Cathryn hauled him back out. It took some maneuvering, bending down to reach him and keeping her too-short skirt in place at the same time.

"Thanks," said Mike, picking up his sunglasses, knocked to the floor in the scuffle. He was angry, obviously, but for some reason he seemed to be trying to hide it.

I looked down into the open locker. The panel of metal on the floor had come loose, bending downwards. It took me a second to figure out why the sight was so weird to me.

Then it clicked.

The locker floor was sinking down way further than it should have. Down into the ground.

I brushed past Cathryn and Mike and stuck one

leg into the locker, testing the floor with my foot. It bent up and down under my shoe, still attached to the walls on two sides.

"Hey, get out of there!" Tank ordered, still not letting go of Peter.

I lifted my foot up off the locker floor.

"Yeah, come on, Jordan," said Mike. "Just back off and –"

I stomped back down again. The dislodged panel came away completely, sending a clang of metal echoing through the corridor. It tumbled downwards, through the floor, into a dark, narrow tunnel.

It was a good five seconds before we heard the muffled sound of the panel hitting the bottom.

Peter twisted under Tank's grip. "What the crap?"

I felt Luke behind me, stretching up to see over my shoulder, and I knew his mind was flashing with exactly the same images as mine was: the tunnels under Phoenix. The ones Shackleton and his people used to get around the town undetected. This had to be part of the same –

SLAM!

Tank shoved me aside and banged the locker shut,

finally letting go of Peter.

Cathryn looked terrified. Whatever all this was, it clearly wasn't meant to be public knowledge.

"You're dead," said Tank, raising his fists. "All three of you. Come anywhere near us again, and I'll –"

"Tank, wait a sec," said Mike. "Let's not do anything stupid."

"Think about who you're talking to, mate," said Peter.

Mike grinned at him, and it looked at least halfway genuine. "You want to come hang out with us this afternoon?"

"What?" said Peter and Cathryn at the same time.

"No way," said Tank, whipping around. "He can't! You know what they told us."

"Tank, shut up!" Cathryn hissed.

"Yeah," said Mike. "I know what they said. Things change, though, don't they? Especially around here." He shrugged. "Up to you, Pete. You ready to give a mate a second chance?"

"So the tunnels mean they're working for Shackleton, right?" I said, my voice low as we crossed the busy food court at the mall that afternoon, keeping an eye out for Peter and the others. Mike's sudden offer of friendship hadn't included Luke and me, but that didn't mean we couldn't listen in. "Question is, why? What are they doing for him that couldn't be done by one of his other thugs?"

Luke shrugged. "Here's what I don't get. If they *are* working for Shackleton, then why did Cat freak out so much when she caught us watching that DVD Bill left us? I mean, if she already knew what Tabitha was –"

"Who says they knew about Tabitha?" I asked. "Look at Peter's dad. He had no idea what he was really involved in."

"Shh!" Luke warned.

Officer Barnett, the guard from Reeve's funeral, was walking towards us, arguing with a small, skinny man with glasses: Arthur van Pelt.

I dragged Luke sideways into a nearby booth, hoping they'd pass by without noticing us, wishing I'd been more careful. But what choice did we have? Speak in public and risk being overheard. Speak in private and risk Shackleton guessing what we were doing.

"Sir," said Barnett behind me, struggling to keep his voice under control, "we're talking about a few groceries. It's not as though –"

"We're talking about four separate breaches of this building's security," snapped van Pelt.

They strode past our booth and I saw Barnett's fingers clenching in frustration.

"Yes, sir," he seethed. "We're working on it."

"I'm not asking you to *work* on it. I'm asking you –" van Pelt kept arguing, but by now they were slipping back out of earshot.

I looked down and realized I was sitting on Luke's hand.

"Sorry," I said, shifting further into the booth.

But Luke was staring off in the opposite direction. Peter and the others were sitting around a table, about twenty meters away. The three boys were demolishing a giant plate of nachos. Cathryn sat back, looking intently at Peter.

"Try to get closer?" said Luke.

I shook my head. They were in the middle of the food court, right out in the open. Didn't matter which direction we came in from, one of them would see us coming.

Which was probably exactly how Mike had planned it.

No point charging in there and ruining Peter's chances of getting anything out of them. I slumped back in my seat. We'd just have to wait for him to fill us in.

"So who do you reckon that guy was that Barnett was arguing with?" asked Luke, watching him head off in the direction of the supermarket.

"You're kidding, right?"

I took it from his blank stare that he wasn't.

"The guy in charge of the mall," I said incredulously. "Arthur van Pelt. From Pryor's phone, remember? I looked him up in the town directory as soon as we found out he was one of Shackleton's people."

"Oh," said Luke. "Good thinking."

"You didn't?"

"Sorry," said Luke, "been kind of busy lately. You know, this apocalypse we're having."

I looked past him at Peter and the others. Mike

was waving his arms around in front of him, telling a story or something. Peter burst out laughing. You could see just by looking at him how much he'd missed hanging out with these guys.

Just don't forget you've got a job to do, I thought.

"So what do you want to do now?" asked Luke, reaching under the table for his bag. "Not much point – Uh-oh."

I tensed, expecting to see Calvin or Pryor or a security officer closing in. But it wasn't any of Shackleton's people.

It was Peter's dad, pushing towards us in his wheelchair. He had a dangerous look in his eyes, the same one Peter always gets a split second before he flies off the handle.

I hadn't spoken to Mr. Weir since before the night at the Shackleton Building. I guess I'd kind of been avoiding him. But I'd seen him, struggling around town, a constant reminder of the grip Shackleton had on us.

Luke moved to get up, but Mr. Weir rolled to a stop next to him, blocking our way out of the booth.

"Uh-uh. No," he said. "No more screwing around."

"Mr. Weir —"

"I know there's something going on in this place," Peter's dad hissed, leaning across the table towards us. "And I know you two know something about it. And neither of you is going anywhere until you tell me *exactly* what the Shackleton Co-operative wants with my son."

Chapter 7

I scanned the food court. There were at least three security guards within sight of us. Three opportunities for this to get extremely messy. But it was worse than that. Shackleton was tracking Peter's dad too. He'd only have to take one look at his computer monitor to guess what we were talking about.

"Mr. Weir, please," I said, "now is not really the –"

"No, I reckon this is the perfect time," said Peter's dad. "Not sure if you kids have noticed, but I've made a bit of a lifestyle change recently." He rapped at the side of his wheelchair. "I reckon it's earned me the right to some bloody answers."

Luke turned to see what I was thinking.

Do we tell him?

Mr. Weir was right. He did have a right to answers. But he also had the right to keep on being alive, and right now it was pretty much one or the other.

"I'm really sorry about what happened," I said. "But why would you think we had anything to do with it?"

"Don't give me that. You think I didn't notice the way you three were limping around last week? You think I don't know what they've done to you?"

Luke forced a puzzled look. His acting skills had come a long way since he arrived here. "Mr. Weir, whatever you think is going on here –"

"Listen, mate." Peter's dad leaned in closer. "If you reckon I'm just going to sit by and wait for those people to –" He moved to stand up, like for a second he'd forgotten what the suppressor had done to his legs. Then he realized what he was doing and slumped back down again.

He swallowed, gazing down into his lap, and for the first time I noticed the unshaven face, the uncombed hair, the bags under the eyes. Little glimpses at the toll the last ten days had taken.

All this guy wanted was to protect his son, and

here we were, hiding the truth from him.

The anger drained out of Mr. Weir's face and he put his head down in his hands. "Stay away," he said, eventually. "You just stay away from him, okay? Please. Whatever this is, just leave him out of it."

I opened my mouth to – to what? Lie to him some more? But then my stomach convulsed and I jerked forward, retching.

My head hit the table and, in that same instant, the sound cut out all across the food court. Every voice, silenced. The lights flickered off. I lifted my head and found myself alone in the mall.

Another one, I thought dizzily. Another flash, or vision, or whatever we were calling them.

I stood up, holding my head, trying to get my bearings. The whole world blurred around me. It was night outside. I could see stars glinting through the glass ceiling.

But which night? Was I seeing something that had already happened, or –?

"Hurry!" said a girl's voice from behind me. I jumped, and the room spun some more. *"Thirty-five seconds!"*

Rattling wheels and jangling metal.

I climbed up and looked over the back of my seat.

Three people were sprinting across the deserted food court, pushing a cart piled up with groceries. They were dressed all in black, with balaclavas over their faces, but I recognized the figures immediately.

Cathryn, Mike and Tank.

I turned my head, following them across the room. But the more I moved, the fuzzier everything got. My stomach gave another pull. I grabbed the back of the seat, steadying myself.

They hurtled towards me, Tank at the back of the cart, Mike and Cathryn holding on at the sides. Mike looked in my direction, staring straight through me.

You're not here, I reminded myself. *It's just a —*

But it wasn't a memory this time. Not my memory, anyway. This was all completely new.

"*Twenty seconds,*" said Cathryn, looking down at a silver stopwatch strapped to her arm.

As they flashed past, I got a better look at the stuff in the cart. All boxes and cans. Nothing perishable.

Bomb shelter food.

Mike had something black sticking out of his

pocket. A notebook or something. He kept reaching back with his free hand to check if it was still there.

"*This way*," he said, pointing across at a set of sliding doors leading out into the park.

"*I know*," Tank grunted, hunched over the cart. "*Shut up and push.*"

"*Ten seconds*," said Cathryn.

They pulled to a stop at the doors.

And they waited.

"*Five seconds.*"

Four. Three. Two. One.

The doors slid open and the three of them hauled the cart outside. I stretched up onto my toes, watching them race away into the park.

The air around me gave another violent shudder, folding in on itself, and I felt my gag reflex kicking in again. I grabbed my stomach, stumbling over backwards, and –

"Jordan – Jordan, you all right?"

The lights flashed on, and the food court exploded with sound. The world kept swirling for another second or two, then straightened itself out again.

Back to reality.

I felt Luke's hands around my arms, holding me up. I'd fallen back on top of him.

"Yeah," I murmured, shuffling back across to my side of the seat.

Head still spinning, I checked the surrounding tables, trying to work out how much of a scene I'd made. There were a couple of curious stares, but it looked like Mr. Weir's wheelchair had mostly blocked me from sight.

"We should get out of here," I said, giving Luke a nudge.

He slid across to the end of the seat. Mr. Weir narrowed his eyes, and I half-expected him to try and stop us, but he looked like he'd used up all his energy on that first outburst. He spun around and wheeled away without another word.

"Sure you're okay?" said Luke, watching him go.

"I'm fine," I whispered. "He could be trouble, though, if – Great. What now?"

Peter was charging up to us. Mike, Cathryn and Tank watched from the table behind him, wearing matching looks of confusion.

He was almost running by the time he got to us,

face wild with anger.

"What the crap do you think you're doing?" he demanded, heading straight for Luke.

"Peter, quiet," said Luke. "You're going to –"

"Stay away from my dad!" snapped Peter. "What, you don't think they've done enough to him already? You want to get him *killed?*"

"Yes, Peter, that's exactly what I'm doing. I'm trying to get Shackleton to kill your dad. That what you want me to say?" Luke's voice was low, but we were still attracting attention.

"Listen," I hissed, desperate to placate Peter before he lost the plot completely, "your dad came up to us, all right? And we denied everything. If you've got a problem, go take it up with him."

Peter's mouth moved again, but no sound came out. His shoulders dropped and he said, "Oh."

"Yeah," I said. "So why don't you get back over there and get on with what you're supposed to be doing?"

If Luke had spoken to him like that, Peter probably would have punched his face in. But if there was an upside to Peter's obsession with me, it was that he was actually willing to hear me out from time to time.

"Right," he mumbled, turning back. "You're right. Sorry."

He headed back to his friends, and Luke and I finally escaped the food court. We started making our way to the other end of the mall, where I was supposed to be meeting Mum to give her a hand with the groceries.

I kept glancing backwards to make sure we weren't being followed. Between my latest vision thing and being tag-teamed by Peter and his dad, it was a miracle we hadn't been dragged away to the security center by now.

"Twice in one day," said Luke.

"Huh?"

"Peter. That's the second time he's blown up at us over nothing. I think he's getting worse."

He stopped walking. Officer Barnett and another guard were patrolling back in our direction. We veered across to Rebirth and pretended to look through a rack of shirts out in front.

"Getting worse?" I said, leaning close to be heard over the pounding music. "You think Peter is – You think this is like my visions, or Jeremy's hand, or –?"

83

I cut myself short, avoiding saying Georgia's name, still not ready to admit that yesterday was anything more than a creepy one-off.

"I dunno," said Luke, picking up a shirt from the rack as Barnett came past. The two officers spotted us standing there and paused. I took a couple of steps further into the shop, faking interest in clothes only Cathryn would wear.

Eventually, they moved on.

"Maybe it's just stress," I said. "His dad and everything."

"Yeah. Maybe."

He put down the shirt and we left the shop.

"Either way, though," he said, "if this keeps happening – I mean, if he keeps losing it like this, we could have a problem."

"Yeah," I sighed. "It would really suck for us to have a problem."

Luke looked like he didn't know whether to smile or say something reassuring. Before he had time to do either, a high voice cut across the mall.

"Jordan!"

Georgia was running over, grinning. She always

84

seemed to pick the most random days to be excited to see me.

Mum was out in front of the supermarket, getting a cart. She narrowed her eyes, like she was debating whether to call Georgia back or not, but in the end she just let her go.

I noticed the puddle on the floor too late – a knocked-over Coke cup that the cleaners hadn't gotten to yet. I called out to Georgia, but her foot had already come down on top of it. She slipped, sprawled forward, and hit the marble floor. Hands first, then her head.

A second of dazed silence, and then the crying started.

Mum and I both ran across to help. But before either of us could reach her, two hands came down and scooped her up.

Arthur van Pelt. He hoisted Georgia into his arms and started patting her on the back.

I broke into a run.

Let her go, you –

I reached them just ahead of Mum. Van Pelt was rocking Georgia back and forth, whispering into her ear. "Shhh … Hey, c'mon, you're all right. You're all right. Look, here's Mum!"

Georgia's a tough kid, and she was already calming down. She turned around in van Pelt's arms, wiping the tears from her eyes with the back of her hand.

"Thanks," said Mum, reaching out to take her from him.

"I'm so sorry about this," said van Pelt, frowning at the spilled Coke. "I'll have someone – Whoa, hey, what's –?"

Georgia was suddenly fighting to get free of him, writhing around like she was being electrocuted. She clawed at van Pelt's face, kicking at him, attacking him with her whole body. Her tears were back with a vengeance. Breath coming in short, terrified gasps.

"Georgia!" said Mum. "Sweetheart, what's –?"

"He wants to hurt everybody!" Georgia screamed, thrusting her arms out towards me. "He wants to hurt everybody!"

Chapter 8

"Seriously, Jordan, she'll be fine," said Peter again. "They're not going to do anything to her."

"She attacked one of the leaders of the Shackleton Co-operative!" I whispered, skirting around the edge of the quad. "She screamed out, 'He wants to hurt everybody!' in front of half the town!"

Peter stooped down to catch a handball that was bouncing towards us. "She's six years old," he said, chucking it back. "Who's going to listen to her?"

"They will," I said. "Because they know she's right."

The question was, what else did they know? Would they think I'd told her about Tabitha? Or did van Pelt know enough to guess that there was something even weirder going on?

Either way, I was dreading the Shackleton Co-operative's next move.

The bell went, and we started cutting across in the direction of the gym. Cathryn, Tank and Mike were already over there, waiting.

Peter had gotten nothing out of them yesterday.

It looked like the only reason they'd invited him along was to try to smooth over the locker incident and convince him how normal and innocent they all were. The most suspicious thing he'd come back with was that Tank had been "scratching his arm a lot."

Brilliant.

Before school this morning, I'd filled Luke in on my latest vision. I'd almost told Peter too, a couple of times, but something kept holding me back. The last thing I needed right now was hearing him go on about how impossible it all was.

Besides, it was hard to see how knowing that Peter's old friends were stealing groceries from the mall was actually useful information. If anything, it made things even more confusing, because why would Shackleton have them stealing from his own supermarket?

Unless it was some kind of test or something. Maybe Shackleton was –

Huh.

I lost track of my thoughts, attention flashing across to the gym. Mike had just twisted around to stick something in his bag.

A black notebook.

The one from my vision.

Maybe yesterday afternoon hadn't been such a waste of time after all.

"Peter," I whispered, grabbing his arm. "That book Mike just put in his bag. Have you ever seen it before?"

Cathryn glanced up and I shut my mouth. She smiled at Peter, then went back to her conversation with Mike and Tank.

Ms. Jeffery appeared at the door and sent us all in to get changed. On the way inside, Peter went over and slapped Mike on the back. "Hey, mate. After school, you guys want to go –?"

"Sorry, man," said Mike. "Homework."

Peter smirked. "Homework?"

"Yeah, it's like school work, but you do it at your house."

"Since when do you do it at all?" said Peter.

Mike started to answer, but by then they'd both turned into the guys' locker room.

I walked across to the girls' and got into my PE uniform as slowly as possible, weighing up my chances of sneaking in and getting Mike's notebook without getting caught.

All around me, the other girls were busy complaining about their mobile phones not working or discussing how wrong it was that Hannah was going out with a guy in Year 8.

Like these were the biggest problems in the world.

I took off my school shirt, careful not to smudge the makeup on my hand. The discolored skin was starting to darken again, but it was still a long way from normal.

Luke would tell you to wait, I thought. *He'd tell you there'd be plenty of other opportunities to get that notebook. No point rushing in there now.*

But what if there weren't other opportunities?

What if this was it?

What if I'd seen that notebook in my vision because I'd *needed* to see it?

I pulled my sports shirt down over my head and saw Cathryn staring at me from across the room. She didn't even try to disguise the scowl on her face. I rolled my eyes and reached for my shorts.

How much do you know? I wondered.

Judging from her reactions to Luke, Peter and me, it definitely didn't seem like Cathryn had the whole picture of what was going on in Phoenix. Shackleton had obviously told them *something* in that letter – but then, who knew how much of it was even true?

And that was another thing: Cathryn's mum, Louisa Hawking, was one of the heads of the Shackleton Co-operative. So why was Shackleton communicating with Cathryn and the others through a locker in the school? Surely it would be easier to just pass their instructions on through her.

Unless not even she was allowed to know what they were up to. If the information he was giving them was so sensitive that he needed to contact them directly.

I watched Cathryn frowning into her compact, brushing at her cheek with the back of her nail.

Not that I had any idea what she was supposed to be doing for Shackleton – but was she really the best he could come up with?

The room eventually began to empty. I finished getting changed and sat down on the bench, pretending to untangle a knot in my shoelaces.

Finally, the last two girls zipped up their bags and headed for the door. I stood in the doorway, watching until they'd left the room completely, then started tiptoeing across to the guys' locker room.

I paused at the door, listening for any signs of life. Empty.

I slipped inside, steadying myself against the nauseating cocktail of spray deodorants, and scanned the room for Mike's bag.

Most of us just used the standard Phoenix High backpack that they gave us when we got here, but Mike had a satchel thing covered in badges and patches. It should have been easy enough to find, but at first I couldn't see any sign of it. I circuited the room. Mike's bag would be somewhere near Tank's. If I could find that –

Ah.

Over in the far corner of the locker room, I spotted a strap of brown fabric poking out from under a pile of discarded clothes and shoes.

Typical, I thought, sliding the bag out from under the mess and shaking off a pair of underpants. I checked the door again and snapped the satchel open.

The notebook was right at the bottom, wedged down underneath all Mike's schoolbooks. I pulled it out and reburied the bag.

I could hear Ms. Jeffery on the other side of the wall, picking teams for whatever we were playing today. It wouldn't be long before someone noticed I was –

Footsteps.

Somebody was coming.

I crept to the door and peered outside.

No one there.

I dashed back out across the gym, figuring it was better to get caught out here than to explain why I was rifling through the guys' bags. Straight through the door to the girls' locker room.

I was halfway to my bag before I saw Cathryn.

I staggered to a stop, almost tripping over myself. She was standing with her back to me, taking off a pair of earrings. I shoved the notebook down the back of my gym shorts.

Cathryn turned around.

She made another face, like she'd just stepped in something, then looked away again.

I sidestepped across the room, keeping my back away from her, and sat down, pretending to search for something in my bag.

Cathryn stuck the earrings in her purse and dropped it into her bag. Then she wheeled around and stormed over to face me.

"Just can't keep your hands to yourself, can you?"

Uh-oh.

"Sorry?" I said, sitting up straighter against the wall.

She stepped closer. "Oh, right. Like you don't know what I'm talking about."

I played dumb. "Cathryn, seriously, what are you trying to –?"

"He's freaking wasted on you," she spat.

And she turned and walked out of the room.

Chapter 9

I was the first one out of the gym at the end of the lesson, more than happy to get clear of Cathryn's continued face-making.

It was insane. The two of us were on opposite sides of a plot to kill seven billion people, and the biggest drama she had with me was that I was hanging out with Peter?

How could she even think there was a problem there? It was one thing for Peter to keep convincing himself that something was going to happen between us, but I would've thought it was pretty clear from the outside that –

Of course.

She was getting all this from him. The way he told it, it was probably only a matter of days before the two of us ran away together.

Like any of us had time to worry about that now.

I leaned back against a wall, waiting for Luke and Peter to hurry up and get changed. I hadn't told them about the notebook yet. We'd spent all of PE on opposing teams, and whenever I got close enough to talk to them, Mike or one of the others seemed to be hovering somewhere in earshot.

It could be nothing, anyway, I reminded myself. *It could be his stamp collection for all you know.*

But it was more than that. More than coincidence. There was a reason I'd found that book.

I walked back over to the door. Tank's voice had suddenly risen up above the noise of the guys' locker room. "Hey – No, don't you – Mate, no, you're a dead man!"

A loud snap, shouts of laughter from the other boys, and Mike came running out of the gym, shirt unbuttoned, bag swinging from his shoulder. Tank ran out after him, tie stretched tight between his hands. He flicked his wrist and caught Mike right between the shoulder blades. Mike shouted, whirled around, and raised his tie into the air to return fire.

"That will do, gentlemen!" called a voice from across the grass.

It was Mr. Hanger. Mike and Tank both started talking at once.

"Come on, sir!"

"We weren't even –!"

"Quiet," said Mr. Hanger. He narrowed his eyes at the gym. "Where is Peter?"

Mike grinned and ran back inside.

"Hey, Pete! Guess who's come to visit?"

A minute later he was back, with Peter and Luke behind him. Peter saw Mr. Hanger and immediately did a one-eighty back towards the gym.

"PETER WEIR!"

"What, sir?" snapped Peter, spinning around again.

Mr. Hanger pulled out a crumpled piece of notebook paper. I recognized it as the "essay" Peter had handwritten in the ten minutes before school started this morning.

Mr. Hanger held up the page and read the first line. *"Why World War II would've been so much more awesome if they'd used robot soldiers."*

"Yeah, sir, about that, I thought your original question was kind of restrictive, so I decided to –"

"Detention, Peter. Now."

"Screw you," Peter muttered, pulling his bag up over one shoulder.

Mr. Hanger snarled. "What was that?"

"I said you're an awesome teacher, sir!" Peter said loudly. "Your comb-over isn't even that noticeable!"

More of the class had arrived by now. Shocked laughter from a few of them.

"Anybody else care to join us?" asked Mr. Hanger, silencing the class. He grunted and turned back to the English building. "This way, Peter."

"He's going to die," I said as soon as they were gone.

Luke sighed. "Which one?"

The bell rang from somewhere inside the gym, and Ms. Jeffery reappeared, shooing the last few students outside. Luke and I headed over to the math building to get our bikes, with Cathryn, Tank and Mike right behind us.

"Crap," said Luke. "Just remembered Mum wanted me to go to the supermarket for her this afternoon."

He dragged his bike out from the rack. "See you tomorrow, okay?"

A tug of disappointment. I thought about calling him back, but there wasn't much I'd be able to say to him with the others still so close. And now that the school day was over, making sure Georgia was okay suddenly felt much more important.

"All right," I said. "See you."

I spun my bike around and headed for the back gate, thinking that if I was quick, I might catch Dad coming in to pick Georgia up. But when I rode down through the primary school, there was no sign of either of them.

I rode straight home and found Dad stooped over his laptop at the kitchen counter. He worked from home on Tuesdays. One of those "great working conditions" the Shackleton Co-operative hoped would help distract its employees from the weirdness of life in Phoenix.

"Hey," I said. "Where's Georgia?"

"She's with Mum. Dr. Montag wanted to give her the once-over after her fall yesterday. Make sure the damage isn't any worse than it looks."

"Oh," I said. My fist tightened around the strap of my backpack. "I think I'll go down there and –"

"How much of that English homework have you done?" said Dad.

"Most of it," I said.

"It's due tomorrow, isn't it?"

"Dad –"

But then I realized he'd just saved me from making a massive mistake.

The suppressor. Shackleton was watching.

If they really were doing something to Georgia, I wouldn't make it halfway to the medical center before I got hauled off by security. And then she'd be in even more trouble than she already was.

Had to be smart about this. I took a breath. "All right."

"She'll be fine, Jordan," said Dad, getting up and putting an arm around me. "It's a concussion at worst. And, hey, compared to our last few visits to the medical center …"

"Yeah," I said, hugging him back. "Just give me a yell when they get back, okay?"

I went to my room, knowing Dad was more

worried about all this than he was letting on. But as usual, he was keeping that to himself. Being strong for his family. More than anyone else, I wished I could tell him what was going on out here.

There was no way I was getting any homework done this afternoon, at least not until Mum and Georgia got back. I sat down on my bed and clawed through my bag for Mike's notebook.

Soft, black, fake-leather cover. Worn around the edges. Bulging in the middle where it looked like he'd glued in a whole bunch of other bits of paper. Elastic strap keeping everything together.

I snapped off the strap and started flipping through the pages.

It was a sketchbook. Page after page of drawings. A map of Phoenix Mall, drawn on graph paper and glued in. Bits of the bush around Phoenix, but nothing I recognized. A few random sketches from around town.

But what really got under my skin was the people.

The same two figures, over and over again. All through the book. Sometimes male, sometimes female, sometimes one of each. But always in pairs. Always dressed in white. They were angelic, almost.

But not wimpy Christmas-card angels with harps and halos and feathery wings. Real angels. The kind that strike you down in awe and terror.

I closed the book, suddenly uneasy.

Don't be stupid, I warned myself. *They're just pictures.* Just pictures that had arrived in my hands thanks to a time-bending supernatural vision.

Voices echoed up the hall from the front of the house, snapping me out of it. Mum and Georgia were home. I shoved the notebook under my pillow and rushed out to see them.

Georgia had sprinted straight through the door and was already stomping up the stairs to her room. Mum came in after her, shooting a weary look at Dad, who was walking down the hall ahead of me.

"Guess who just lost their job," she said.

Dad put his hands around her waist. "What? Oh no."

"Dr. Montag wants me to finish up at the preschool this week," said Mum. She sighed, moving past him towards the family room. "Maternity leave. He doesn't want to take any chances with the baby."

Yeah, I thought darkly, following them. *I bet.*

But if this was the first thing Mum mentioned as she walked through the door, that had to mean nothing too weird had happened at the medical center.

Mum crashed onto the couch and Dad sat down next to her.

"Good that the doc is playing it safe," he said unconvincingly.

"Yeah," said Mum. "And if I do only have eight and a half weeks to go … I mean, when you think about it that way, it's not that much more leave than I'd normally be taking. I guess it makes sense."

Dad shook his head. "Nothing about this makes sense."

"What did they say about Georgia?" I asked, settling onto the couch opposite them.

But before Mum could answer, Georgia came bowling into the room, carrying a heart-shaped wooden box with a photo of her and Grandma set into the top. She'd gotten it as a going-away present right before we came here.

Georgia held the box out to Mum, fixing her with a stern look. "Remember, I only want green and purple and pink this time."

"Right," said Mum.

Georgia plonked herself down at Mum's feet. Mum handed the heart box to Dad. He flipped it open and started sorting elastics, while she got started redoing Georgia's braids.

I curled up on the couch and closed my eyes. Clearly, Montag had been checking for more than just a concussion, but he'd sent Georgia home in one piece, so that was one less thing to panic about, at least for tonight.

"It's good that you've finished feeling sick in the mornings," said Georgia out of nowhere, breaking the silence. I opened my eyes.

She was looking up at Mum.

It took Mum a minute to respond and when she did, it was hesitant. "How did you know that, sweetheart?"

"You just said it!" Georgia twisted up her face, like Mum was being slow on purpose.

Mum stopped braiding. "Georgia, I wasn't even speaking."

Georgia turned around again and leaned her head back, waiting for Mum to get back to work.

"I know," she said. "You don't have to anymore."

I had another look through Mike's sketchbook before I went to sleep, trying to figure out what it all meant. Trying to distract myself from worrying about Georgia.

Mum and Dad had let the moment slip past without any more comment, but I could tell the weirdness of it hadn't been lost on them.

I stared down at yet another pair of carefully sketched men in white, my eyes blurring with exhaustion. The longer I looked at them, the stronger the urge to check over my shoulder and make sure I wasn't being watched.

Get a grip.

I snapped the sketchbook shut and flicked off my bedside light.

Nightmares had been a part of life ever since all of this started. But tonight I had new enemies. Faceless, white-robed figures, chasing me through the bush. Hunting me. The figures flickered, real one second, hand-drawn the next, but always right behind me. I pressed forward, grass rising, trees closing in on all sides, and suddenly I was out over the lip of a giant, flaming crater. I tumbled forward, down into the bottomless darkness –

And then all of it was gone.

Solid ground under me. I was back in my room.

I opened my eyes, drifting up from sleep, trying to get my bearings.

Cold air.

Had I left the window open?

I glanced up at the clock. Just before midnight.

And then suddenly the clock flashed off, blocked by a dark shape slipping past in front of it.

There was someone in my room.

Chapter 10

The silhouette moved on, melting into the darkness of the bedroom, and for a moment I lost track of it. I froze, trying and failing to steady my breathing, disjointed images rushing at me. Knives and cold eyes and grasping hands and gunshots and pillows held down over my –

Shuffling noises from over near my desk. Barely audible. Whoever this was, they were used to getting around undetected.

I closed my eyes for just a second, trying to refocus. Only one way I was getting out of this. I eased out from the covers, slow and quiet, letting my intruder keep on thinking I was asleep.

More movement. There was someone crouched down there on the floor.

A tiny trickle of relief pierced through my chest. The figure was small. Or human-sized, anyway. No billowing white robes. Nothing glowing.

Not that there weren't plenty of humans around who were more than capable of doing me in.

The intruder rose slowly, his back still to me, stretching up to investigate my desk.

I pushed myself up into a sitting position, then swung my legs around and brought them down onto the carpet.

There was a tiny thud as my visitor accidentally bumped into my desk chair. I gasped, startled, then froze again, sure I'd just given myself away.

The intruder hesitated for a second, then gently pushed the chair aside and continued canvassing the desk.

I stood up and crept over, pausing after each step.

Three meters away.

Two meters.

One.

The figure straightened up, backing away from

the desk. His head began to turn, but I was already jumping forward. I brought one arm down across his neck, the other around his stomach, trying to keep his hands down.

Then I saw the black hair poking down from the back of his balaclava.

Mike.

He staggered back, writhing and twisting, trying to jerk his body clear. Squeezing him tighter with both arms, I angled my foot around to kick him behind the knees. He stumbled, grunting again, but stayed standing, throwing his head back, trying to catch me in the teeth. I dodged left, kicking him again, and he finally fell, crashing roughly onto his knees beside my bed.

He grunted as the impact jarred his knees, and again as I brought my weight down on top of him, pinning his chest to the carpet.

Mike kept right on struggling. "Get – off, you –!"

"Shh!" I drove an elbow down between his shoulder blades. "You really want my dad coming in here?"

Mike stopped struggling. "Where is it?" he hissed.

Keeping one hand planted firmly on Mike's back,

I reached up under my pillow and brought out the sketchbook.

"So Cathryn knows how to put two and two together after all, huh?" I whispered, yanking off the elastic one-handed.

"Oi, careful!" said Mike. "You do anything to that book and I'll –"

"Seriously, Mike. Just stop talking."

I'd seen way too much real danger in this place to be intimidated by a weedy kid in a balaclava.

I held the book up to the moonlight streaking in through the window, opened it to a particularly detailed picture of the people in white robes, and slapped it down in front of his face.

"Tell me who these guys are and I'll let you go."

"Uh, Jordan," said Mike. "Kind of dark in here. How am I supposed to –?"

"Shut up, Mike. You know who I'm talking about."

His eyes dropped to the carpet. "They're no one," he said. "I made them up. What, you think there are real people who look like –?"

Bang.

The room flooded with light.

110

A giant shadow fell down on us from the doorway.
Mike swore.

It was Dad.

He stood there for a minute, taking in the scene.
His fifteen-year-old daughter, pinning a masked
intruder to her bedroom floor in the dead of night.

"Jordan, who –?"

I scrambled up, retrieving the sketchbook from
under Mike's nose. Mike got up too, brushing himself
off.

Just in time for Dad to grab him by the arm.

He pulled the balaclava off Mike's face and stared
down at him. That was not a stare you wanted to be
on the wrong side of.

"What's your name, kid?" asked Dad.

Mike didn't answer. He shook his head, flicking
the hair back out of his face.

"All right," said Dad, pulling him in the direction
of the door. "Well, I'm sure security will be able to
figure it out."

"No, Dad, wait! He's not –" I bit my lip. "He
hasn't done anything. Mike's just – a friend."

Surprise flashed across both their faces.

But if Calvin found out I was having visitors in the middle of the night, it would be all he needed to convince Shackleton to pull the pin on my suppressor.

"A friend," Dad repeated.

"Yeah," said Mike, seizing the opportunity. "I'm really sorry, Mr. Burke. It was stupid to come here so late, but I just – Jordan has an art project of mine that I really needed to get back."

He glanced down at the sketchbook in my hand.

I scowled at him.

Well played, I thought grudgingly, holding out the book. Dad came over and took it from me. He flipped through the pages, then snapped the book shut and handed it to Mike.

"Thanks," said Mike, moving towards the door. "Well, I guess I should probably get out of your hair." He stared up at Dad's shaven head. "I mean –"

Dad stepped across to block the doorway. "This isn't going to happen again," he said, crossing his arms. "Is it, Mike?"

Mike shook his head.

"Good. Come with me."

"He walked him home?" said Luke.

"Yep," I said. "And this morning, me and Dad had a really fun chat about whether or not I'm ever allowed to have a boy over to the house again."

"And?" said Peter. "Are you?"

"That's ... still being negotiated," I said, pretending not to hear the obsessiveness in his voice.

Mr. Larson came past, dropping a copy of *The Strange Case of Dr. Jekyll and Mr. Hyde* in front of each of us.

"You know, you really need to get some bars or something for that window," said Luke.

"Yeah, no kidding."

Across the classroom, Mike and the others were deep in conversation. Mike kept glancing over at us when he thought I wasn't watching. He looked like he hadn't slept.

Had I really seen anything that incriminating?

"So what was in that sketchbook, anyway?" asked Luke, obviously wondering the same thing.

"Here," I said, unfolding a bit of paper and flattening it out on the table. As soon as Dad had left the house last night, I'd scribbled down as many of Mike's drawings as I could remember. "This is only some of it, but –"

"The locker," said Peter, pointing at a crooked rectangle with a door on it. "Right? The one from the other day."

"Yeah," I said. "And he had a list of dates next to it, back to the beginning of April, all crossed out."

"April," said Peter. "That's –"

"Right around the time they all went off the deep end?" I said. "Yeah, that's what I thought."

"Who are those guys?" asked Luke, pointing at my drawing of the two people in white.

I shook my head. They'd definitely lost something in translation. The sizes and shapes were all about right, but I hadn't come close to capturing the creepiness of Mike's figures.

"Dunno," I said. "Mike said he made them up."

"All right, ladies and gentlemen," said Mr. Larson, returning to the front of the room. "Dr. Jekyll and Mr. Hyde – I assume you've heard these names before?"

A few hands went into the air.

"Great! Then let's figure out what we know so far."

Mr. Larson launched into a brainstorming session, typing people's suggestions up on the interactive whiteboard.

I smoothed my page out on the table again and racked my brain for any other missing details. The drawings of the bushland were the hardest. I was sure they'd all been detailed enough in the sketchbook, but by now I couldn't picture much more than a mess of grass and trees.

There was only one that I remembered clearly, and I'd already started drawing it: trees all along the back, a bunch of giant rocks on one side, and –

"Jordan, what about you?" asked Mr. Larson.

"I'm not sure, sir," I said, scanning the board for a clue to what we were talking about.

Mr. Larson smiled. "Not sure about the answer, or not sure about the question?"

"Um … both," I said, quickly looking down at my copy of the book. "Sorry, sir."

But as soon as he'd moved on, I rummaged for a blue pen and started scribbling some water into my drawing, trickling along in front of the rocks.

I hadn't even lifted the pen before Peter snatched the paper away from me.

"Is this a lake?" he asked.

"How should I know?" I whispered. "I'm only drawing what Mike drew."

"I know where this is! We found it ages ago, when we were first –" Peter stopped mid-sentence, like he'd suddenly realized what he was saying. "Ah, crap."

"What?"

He put his head down on the table. "You're going to make me show you where it is, aren't you?"

Chapter 11

"And you're sure they're at the mall?" said Luke as we rode along the north edge of town that afternoon.

"Yes," said Peter. "I told you, Mike asked me to come with them. But, hey, why would I want to hang out with my old mates when I could be riding into the Forbidden Forest with you guys?"

He grinned at me, veering left onto an all-too-familiar dirt track leading out into the bush.

I didn't return the smile. I was grateful for his help, obviously, but I had to be careful how I showed it. I said, *Thanks for coming,* and he heard, *Let's get married.*

I pedaled after him, pushing down the foreboding that hit me as we left the concrete path. Things hadn't exactly gone well for us on our previous trips out here. And that was before we got injected with the suppressors. Before Shackleton started tracking our every move.

This is different, I told myself.

I couldn't put my finger on why exactly. But that drawing of Mike's – It was more than just by chance that I'd seen it, that I'd been able to remember what it looked like, that Peter had known where it was.

Besides, we weren't trying to break into a Co-operative outpost this time.

At least, that's what I was starting to believe. Because the more I thought about the stuff Mike had drawn in his sketchbook, the more I noticed the stuff he *hadn't* drawn.

There'd been no pictures of closed-down airports or secret warehouses or giant prison walls. No hidden trapdoors or tunnels under the town. No screaming test subjects or piles of tattered clothes.

It was like they had no idea about any of it.

Whatever this was, it was ... something else.

Trees blurred past on either side. Looking ahead, I saw someone riding by in the opposite direction. A guy about my dad's age. I'd seen him around town. He glared at us on his way past, like he was sure we were up to something.

But even with the occasional cyclist staring us down, we'd decided it was worth staying on the public bike paths for as long as possible. The less time we spent bush-bashing, the less opportunity we gave Shackleton to wonder what we were up to.

"Hey, check it out," said Peter, slowing down a bit.

Up ahead, all along the left-hand side of the road, the bushland had been cordoned off with Shackleton Co-operative security tape.

DANGER: DO NOT CROSS

The tape stretched out alongside us for about a hundred meters, then ran away into the bush.

"The explosion site," I said. I could just make out the edge of the fire-damaged area through the maze of trees.

"Don't even think about it," said Peter, speeding up again. "One death wish at a time."

A minute or two later, he pulled to a stop on the right-hand side of the road.

"This it?" asked Luke, following him over.

"Yeah," said Peter. "I think so."

"You think so?"

"Look, mate, feel free to take over the navigating if you reckon –"

Peter broke off. He wheeled his bike a bit further into the bush, and bent down at the base of a tree.

"Crap," he breathed.

I followed after him, peering over his shoulder. Sitting at his feet, wide open and half-buried in the dried mud, was a rusty silver cash box.

We'd been here before.

"The Tabitha DVD," said Peter. "This is where – We were standing right here."

Screaming, disintegrating faces flashed in front of me. Skin bubbling. Eyes –

I shook it off.

"Guess that explains how Cat found us," said Luke. "If they've been coming back out here …"

"We should get moving," I said, looking around for somewhere to hide my bike.

"Wait," said Luke.

I stopped. "Yeah?"

"Are we sure we really want to do this?"

"Mike drew that picture for a reason," I said. "Whatever's going on out there, we need to know about it."

"Do we?" asked Luke. "I mean, we don't even know what we're looking for. And what if it does have something to do with Shackleton? He knows exactly where we are. If he sees us creeping out to something he's built out here ..." He trailed off.

I glanced sideways at Peter, standing a few steps back from us, still working out whose side he was on.

"You're right," I said. "It's a risk. Of course it is. But what other choice do we have?"

"I dunno. I just – I want to make sure we're thinking." Luke slumped down across the handlebars of his bike. "You know what happens if we screw up again."

I thought of Peter's dad, rolling away from us in his wheelchair. Broken.

Reeve, dead on the floor.

And the words Shackleton had left us with.

I'm afraid that, next time, it will be someone you truly care about.

"So are we going or what?" Peter asked me.

Luke sighed and pulled his bike in from the road. "Yeah," he said. "We're going."

Peter stared at him. "Mate, you're the one who –" He gave up, shaking his head. "All right. Whatever. This way."

We stashed our bikes in some scrub, and Peter led us away into the bush. He moved slowly, pausing every few meters to look around, like he still wasn't quite sure where he was going.

I fell back a couple of steps, letting Luke catch up. We trudged through the foot-high grass, eyes darting to the ground to keep from tripping on the tree roots snaking underneath.

Luke's brow was creased in the same torn expression he wore whenever we decided to go through with something like this. His help meant all the more, knowing how much he didn't want to be here.

"Thanks," I whispered.

Luke shrugged. "You would've gone without us anyway, right?"

"Yeah, but still."

"And if you die, then Peter and me have to save the world all by ourselves," he said. "How exactly do you see that working out?"

I smiled. "Good point."

Peter turned around, a little way ahead of us, and I took a quick sidestep away from Luke.

"Oi – shut up," Peter said. "We're almost there."

We pushed on, clambering over the giant gray wrecks of fallen trees that sprawled out of the grass.

I still couldn't figure this bush out. There were some huge trees out here. Some of them had to be hundreds of years old. But on the other side of the concrete wall that surrounded this place, there was nothing but wasteland for miles around.

So where did it all come from? How does a massive circle of bushland just spring up in the middle of nowhere?

We came to the top of a little hill, and Peter stopped again.

"Here," he said, crouching down.

Luke and I crept up behind him. Peering down through the grass, I saw still, brown water stretching out on the other side of the rise. A lake, maybe fifty meters across.

We waited, listening.

Nothing but frogs and birds.

"Let's go have a look," I said.

I straightened up and started slinking down the far side of the rise. A bit further on, I could see a giant rocky mound stretching up on the shore to our right. The boulders from Mike's drawing.

The trees grew thickly all around the lake, making it hard to see much beyond the shore on the opposite side, but from what I could tell, there was no sign that Shackleton's people had ever set foot in this place.

Luke and Peter followed me down.

"So this is the place, right?" said Peter, searching the trees.

"Definitely," I said.

We were standing almost exactly where Mike must have been when he drew the picture.

So what were we supposed to be looking at?

What had brought him out here in the first place?

"Have a look around the other side?" Luke suggested.

"Yeah – hold on."

I took off my backpack and pulled out a little blanket and what was left of our lunches. I spread the blanket out on the ground, scattered the trash on top.

If Shackleton *did* send security after us, hopefully this would convince them that we didn't want any trouble. Nothing wrong with a few kids enjoying an innocent picnic, right?

"Okay," I said, slinging my bag back over my shoulders. "Let's go."

We walked along the shore, weaving in and out of the trees. But if anyone was up to something out here, they'd been careful to cover their tracks. All we found was more of the same water and mud and bush.

By the time we'd gotten three quarters of the way around the lake, the most exciting thing that had happened was Luke almost falling in.

We reached the place where the rocks rose up against the shore. They pressed right up to the water's edge, blocking our way.

I stared back over at the shore where we'd started.

There had to be something I wasn't seeing.

"Well ..." said Luke. "What do you reckon?"

"Maybe it's mole people," said Peter. He picked up a stone and sent it skimming across the surface of the lake. "We should keep an eye out for burrows on our way back."

125

"We need to keep going," I said, ignoring him.

"How?" said Luke. "There's no way around ... the ..."

He trailed off, eyes fixed on the rock face.

I stepped closer to him. "What is it?"

Luke grabbed on to a tree and leaned out over the water. "Look!" he said, pointing to a shadowy shape on the rock.

"Yeah, mate," said Peter, patting him on the shoulder. "No way around. We get it."

At first, I couldn't tell what Luke was getting at either.

But then a little gust of wind sent the water lapping against that section of the rock and I realized I was looking at more than just a shadow.

A slow grin crept across my face.

"It's a cave."

Chapter 12

This was it.

This was why we were here.

"Okay," I said, shrugging off my backpack and shoving it into some bushes, "if we're going to go check it out, we should probably leave our –"

"Whoa, Jordan. Wait," said Peter. "How are we even supposed to get there? The water goes right up to the entrance."

"So? It's like fifteen meters – and the lake's probably not even that deep."

Peter bent down to feel the water.

Luke just looked at me like I was crazy.

"Come on," I said. "The world is ending and you

two are worried about a little swim?"

"It's *cold*," said Peter.

"All right, fine," I said, pulling off my shoes. "I'll go over first, and then I'll call you if there's anything in there."

I got rid of my socks, put my shoes back on again, then took off my sweater and threw it to Luke.

I turned back to the water's edge and stepped in.

The bottom of the lake was slick with mud. I slid, almost going over backwards. Peter put out a hand to save me, but I steadied myself and stepped out of his reach.

It *was* cold. And deeper than I'd thought.

After only a few steps, I was in up to my waist, school skirt dragging around my legs.

"How is it?" asked Luke.

"It's great," I shivered.

I dived forward, swimming the rest of the way. Better to get this over with quickly.

By the time I reached the cave, it was almost too deep to stand. Reaching out through the muddy water, I felt a rock slope leading up to the entrance. I tried to claw my way up, but the whole thing was thick with slime and I couldn't get a foothold.

Then I saw the rope. A thick cord, almost the same color as the rock, stretching down into the water from somewhere inside the cave. I reached across, grabbed the rope, and pulled myself up the slope, back onto dry land.

Still holding on, I leaned back out to see the others. "Guys, come on!"

A pause.

Then a sigh from Peter. "Really?"

"Yes!" I said. "Hurry up!"

I watched until I was sure they were actually coming, then went back to investigating the cave.

The rope was attached to a big steel loop, bolted down to the stone floor. The metal was starting to rust, but it still didn't look like it had been here for more than a year or so.

Splash!

There was a shout from outside, and then Peter started swearing at the top of his lungs. I picked up the rope again, swung back out from the cave and shouted, "Are you okay?"

"No!" Peter yelled. "It's freaking cold!"

He and Luke were both waist-deep in the lake, shirts off, arms above their heads, taking tiny, cringing steps down into the water.

I sighed and left them to it.

A couple of meters in, just far enough to be half-hidden in shadow, the cave opened up a bit, into a cavern about the size of my bedroom. I walked in, squinting in the dim light.

Little blurs of white hovered in front of me. At first, I thought it was just my eyes adjusting. But then I realized what I was looking at.

Candles. Dozens of them, all over the cavern. They lined the walls, standing on little ledges cut into the rock. They were all unlit, but their wicks were black and they had little streams of hardened wax running down the sides.

It couldn't have been long since people were here.

A giant stone sat in the middle of the room. Two meters across, flat on top. Dotted with even more candles. A table.

There were chairs too. Three smaller stones, set around the big one.

I shivered again, but I was pretty sure it had

nothing to do with the freezing water this time.

This place was like something out of a cult.

The white-robed figures from Mike's sketchbook swam back into my mind. My eyes swept the cavern again, making sure I was alone.

I heard more splashing and arguing outside, and Luke and Peter finally appeared, hugging themselves against the cold.

"Whoa," said Peter, stepping into the cavern. "What the crap is all this?"

"Dunno," I said. "Not exactly Shackleton's style, though, is it?"

I paced around to the far side of the table, seeing if there were any tunnels or anything, but it looked like this was it.

Luke came in and sat down on one of the stone chairs. He stared up at the ceiling.

"This is … not what I was expecting."

"What do you think it's for?" I asked. "I mean, it can't just be –"

The ground shifted and I staggered sideways. Around the cavern, the candles started swirling, blurring together.

"Jordan!" said Peter, rushing over.

I turned, dizzily, wondering how he could be so steady on his feet. But then I felt the familiar rush of nausea and –

Peter disappeared, mid-step. Luke too.

All around me, the candles grew taller and burst into life, casting an eerie, dancing glow across the cavern, lighting up the three hunched figures who had suddenly appeared around the stone table: Mike, Cathryn and Tank.

They were dressed in their black mall-robbing outfits again, minus the balaclavas.

And they were blindfolded.

No one moved.

They just sat there in silence.

And judging by their almost-dry clothes, they'd been waiting for a while.

I took a step closer. The cavern blurred again, but not violently. Movement seemed to be getting easier each time. Like my body was getting used to the flashes.

Sitting on the table in the middle of all the candles was a battered old alarm clock.

10:59 p.m.

Tank shifted on his seat. "*They're gone,*" he whispered. "*They've got to be gone by –*"

"*Shh!*" said Mike. "*Just wait.*"

And the cavern went silent again.

I moved a bit further around the table, bracing myself as the world swirled to catch up. I looked around, skin rippling with goose bumps, but it seemed like Tank was right: whoever else had been in here, they were long gone now.

Cathryn reached up to brush a strand of hair out of her face, then flinched in her seat as a harsh beeping split the cavern.

The alarm clock.

11 p.m.

Mike undid his blindfold and got up to switch the clock off.

"*All right,*" he said, sitting back down again. "*Now.*"

Cathryn and Tank ripped off their blindfolds.

Without another word, all three of them pulled up their sleeves to look at their right shoulders.

"*Yes!*" said Mike, grinning uncontrollably. Obsessively.

"*Awesome,*" said Tank. "*This is so freaking awesome.*"

Cathryn still didn't speak. She had a kind of awed expression on her face.

Each of them was staring down at an identical tattoo, still red, raw and swollen where the needle had gone in.

Black circles with spirals in the middle.

The same shape that had cost Jeremy a beating back at school.

"*This is really happening,*" said Cathryn.

"*'Course it's happening,*" said Mike, the glint in his eye slipping over from excited to manic. "*Why do you think they call it destiny?*"

"Are you kidding?" I said, knowing they couldn't hear me. "What's that supposed to mean?"

"*We should go,*" said Tank, getting up.

"*Yeah,*" said Mike. "*They said –*"

The cavern started rolling again.

I felt something tugging at me, dragging me back.

"Jordan … Jordan, c'mon …"

"No," I said, stomach churning. "Wait!"

The world turned inside out, tearing itself to

pieces. The candles blew out.

Luke was shaking my arm, like I'd been asleep and he was trying to wake me.

I stumbled away from him, rubbing my eyes. If moving around inside the visions was getting easier, flashing in and out was only getting more painful.

"You should have left me," I said. "I saw Mike and the others. They're –"

"Yeah, we noticed that too," said Peter. There was an edge to his voice, like he'd just been sprung by a teacher.

"Huh …?"

I opened my eyes.

Cathryn, Tank and Mike were still there.

Chapter 13

No, I thought, getting my head back together. *Not still here. They're here again.*

Standing at the entrance to the cavern. Drenched from the lake and dressed in their uniforms. Mostly, anyway. Mike and Tank had their shirts off. Big square band-aids on their right arms, covering the tattoos.

I could see Mike's mind whirring, searching for the best way to play this. Cathryn stood behind him, watching.

Tank, on the other hand, clearly wasn't interested in the subtle approach. He charged into the cavern, grabbed Luke – who was closest – by the arm, and growled, *"Get – out."*

"Hang on, man," said Mike, moving to stop him. "Let's just – Let's just figure this out."

Tank looked confused, although that was hardly unusual. He backed off and sat down on one of the stone chairs.

Mike's eyes shot between Luke, Peter and me, calculating. He started pacing around, like he was taking in the cavern for the first time.

"What is this place?" he asked "What are you doing out here?"

It would've been worth a shot if Tank hadn't already been about to rip Luke's arm off. And if I hadn't just seen them using the cavern as a *Twilight Zone* tattoo parlor.

"Show me your arm," I said, sidestepping in front of Mike.

"What?" His face went red. "No. Screw you. Why would I –?"

I slammed him up against the wall, sending candles toppling down. "Seriously, Mike, you want me to knock you down again? Just show me."

"Whoa, Jordan, relax," said Peter. "He's had that band-aid on his arm for ages. It's nothing –"

137

Tank jumped up from his seat and strode over to break it up. Luke, who seemed to have guessed that this had something to do with my vision, ran across and grabbed Tank from behind.

"Oi!" Tank swung a fist back over his shoulder, catching Luke in the side of the head. Luke staggered back against the stone table.

I ripped off the band-aid.

Mike scrambled to cover his arm. Too late.

"Mate ..." said Peter, moving in for a closer look. "Where did you *get* that?"

"Yeah, Mike," I said, leaning on him. "Where'd you get it? Couldn't have been here, could it?"

"How the crap did you know that?" asked Tank.

Mike gritted his teeth. "*Tank!*"

"Who gave them to you?" I asked. "Those guys in white?"

"No one."

"Same no one who keeps posting love notes to you in that locker?" said Peter.

"Pete, come on," said Tank, rounding on him. "Whose side are you on?"

"Here's the deal," I said, turning my attention

back to Mike. "You either tell us what we want to know, or this secret hideout of yours stops being secret."

"And what about your secret?" said Cathryn, speaking for the first time, strolling across from the other end of the cavern.

"Cathryn," Mike warned.

But Cathryn wasn't hearing it. "That video," she said, turning to Peter. "Those people you killed. How would it be if the whole town found out about *that?*"

I let go of Mike.

Cathryn might have come to a completely idiotic conclusion about that DVD, but if she and the others went back and started talking about Tabitha, Shackleton would know exactly where they'd gotten it from.

"No," said Luke, still holding his jaw. "Cathryn, you can't."

"Yeah, seriously, Cat," said Peter. "You don't want to do that."

"Then you probably don't want to go threatening us either," said Mike, stepping away from the wall and brushing himself off.

I got out of his way, and he went over to Tank.

We stood there, all six of us, just eyeing each other across the cavern.

Now what?

The silence stretched out.

Mike's brow furrowed, like he was concentrating on something.

"Well," said Peter finally, clasping his hands together. "I think we've all made some excellent progress today. Why don't we –?"

"Shh!" said Mike.

Peter took one step towards him, then froze. "Crap."

Voices out at the lake.

Mike turned and ran. I bolted after him.

We reached the mouth of the cave at the same time, and the two of us almost went crashing over into the water. I grabbed hold of the rock wall, getting my footing again.

The sun was starting to set, casting an orange glow over the surface of the lake. Mike leaned out, scanning the area, then hauled his body back into the cavern. "Uh-oh."

I crouched and peered across the water.

Officer Calvin and two of his security team. I had to crane my neck to see them around the rock face. They were thirty or forty meters away, back where we'd started, staring down at the fake picnic we'd left on shore.

"You freaking moron!" hissed Peter, suddenly behind us, and it took me a second to realize he was talking to Mike. "You led them right here!"

"We're not the ones who left our crap lying around for anyone to find," said Mike, as one of the guards started kicking through the scraps on the blanket.

But obviously none of that was the real reason they'd shown up.

It was us. Shackleton had seen that we'd stopped here, and he'd sent security to sort us out.

Calvin skulked around like a wild dog, itching for an excuse to do something horrible to us.

"Ugh," said Peter. "I liked it so much better when he was crippled."

"Back inside," I whispered, dragging Mike and Peter with me.

"Hey – no – we need to get out of here," said Peter. "If he finds us …"

"What, you think you're going to swim back over without being seen?" I said. "Because you weren't exactly stealthy the first time."

"Calm down," said Tank. "No one even knows about this place."

"We found it okay," Peter muttered.

But Tank was kind of right. The Co-operative couldn't have known what he and the others were doing in this place, or else they would've put a stop to it. If we were lucky, Calvin would give up soon enough, and –

"They're coming!" said Mike, back at the entrance. "They're walking around the lake."

But since when had we ever been lucky?

I turned to Luke. "How well did you two hide your bags and stuff?"

Luke cringed. "Pretty well."

Great.

I got down low and crept over to look out at the shore again. Calvin and his men were already halfway around the lake. Their eyes were mostly on the bushland, which was good, but they'd still have no problem finding the cave if we gave them a reason to look over here.

And unfortunately, it looked like we already had.

There was a blotch of white gleaming out from under one of the bushes. The corner of a shirt, somehow even more noticeable in the fading light.

"*Pretty well,*" I muttered.

Nothing we could do about it now.

Mike was still at the entrance. He bent down, wrapping his fingers around the rope trailing down into the water.

"What are you doing?" I hissed.

"Pulling it in. They'll see it, otherwise."

"What they'll *see,*" I said, grabbing his wrists, "is that rope sending ripples across the whole lake."

Mike stared at me for a minute, not impressed that I was telling him what to do.

Then he released his grip on the rope.

I let go of his hands, breathing again.

"All right," he said, following me back into the cavern. "How are *you* getting us out of this, then?"

"I'm not," I said. "We're going to wait here until they go. Nothing else we can do."

"Yeah there is," said Cathryn, turning to Mike. "*We* haven't done anything wrong. We should just hand these guys over and –"

"And what?" said Mike. "Just invite them into the cave? How happy do you think the overseers are going to be if the town finds out about this place?"

"Be quiet," said Luke. "All of you – please. Jordan's right. We need to just sit tight and wait for this to blow over. We can all go back to hating each other tomorrow."

Silence. I figured that was as close as we were going to get to an agreement.

"Everyone move to the back of the cavern," I said. "I'm going to go keep an eye on them."

Mike stepped forward, but I held up a hand.

"*I'm* going to keep an eye on them."

He let it go, and I tiptoed up the tunnel alone.

I crawled the last few meters, sticking to the shadows, trying to catch a glimpse of Calvin on the shore. But they'd already come around too far. No way to see them without swinging out on the rope again.

Which meant they had to be right where we were standing when Luke had seen the cave. Right on top of all of our bags and clothes.

Close enough for me to make out their voices.

"Sir," called one of the guards. "Found something over here."

My fingernails dug into the ground.

No.

Quiet from across the water.

When the other guard spoke, he sounded unimpressed.

"A shirt."

"Give it to me," Calvin barked.

More quiet.

Adrenaline coursed through my body, fueling me up to run away or fight. Useless energy when I couldn't do either.

Finally, Calvin spoke again. "It's not theirs."

"Sir – How do you know?"

"Look at it," Calvin spat. "It's enormous."

Tank, I realized.

I glanced over my shoulder, half-tempted to go back there and kill him myself.

"Sir," said the guard who'd spotted the shirt, "there's a boy in their year who's probably about this –"

"I'm aware of that," said Calvin.

"Yes, sir. Maybe he was with them."

"Obviously he was with them."

The officer seemed to sense that Calvin was losing patience. "Yes, sir," he tried again. "Obviously – But – Maybe he was helping them."

"No," said Calvin, and now it sounded like he was talking to himself. "No, they know better than that."

He paused again.

I felt my stomach twist with every break in the conversation, terrified that one of them had noticed the cave.

"Sir," the officer said slowly, "this would be a lot easier if you told us what you think these children are up to."

"Making your life easy is not a priority of mine, Miller," said Calvin coldly.

"No, sir."

I waited to hear Calvin's next orders, but the conversation seemed to be over. Whatever they were doing now, they were doing it quietly.

In my head, I saw Calvin pressing a finger to his lips. Pointing out to the cave. Stepping into the water. Waving at his men to follow.

I forced myself to focus, listening for any splashing in the lake.

Nothing.

Nothing, for what seemed like forever.

And then I saw them.

Over on the opposite shore, walking back the way they had come.

They were leaving.

I pulled my body up a bit higher, shifting around to track their path around the lake.

Calvin and his men were almost back at our picnic site now. Almost gone.

Then Calvin stopped.

He turned, staring across at the rock face.

I shrank back into the shadows.

Calvin watched the rocks, like he knew he was missing something. Looking nearly straight at me.

Then he moved on again, leading the others away into the bush.

Chapter 14

I found Luke waiting in line at the bakery the next morning. He looked wrecked. The stress of yesterday would've been more than enough to explain it, but I knew that wasn't the reason. I'd seen that battered look before – usually early in the morning, and always when he thought no one was watching.

He'd been up thinking about his dad again.

Mourning. Worse than mourning.

Everything we knew told us Luke's dad had been tracked down in Sydney and killed. But what if he hadn't? What if he'd somehow managed to escape whoever Shackleton had sent after him? How long could Luke keep holding on to that hope?

"Hey," I said, hopping off my bike and joining the line behind him. "You all right?"

Luke thought about it. "Alive," he said. He nodded at the counter in front of us. "You want anything?"

"I'll get it," I said, reaching for my purse. "We're already even."

"Jordan, seriously, it's the end of the world," said Luke. "Tell me what you want for breakfast."

I negotiated him down to a hot chocolate, and we wandered up the street towards school. Still no sign of Peter, which was probably good, given what Luke had just done. Not that it had meant anything. But that wouldn't stop Peter reading plenty into it.

"What about you?" asked Luke through a mouthful of croissant. "You doing okay?"

"I'm fine," I said. "It's just – I really thought we were going to find out something useful yesterday. All we got was more questions and another brush with death."

Luke shrugged. "That's not exactly unusual for us, is it?"

"Yeah, but … yesterday was supposed to be different," I said.

"Supposed to be."

"I don't know," I sighed. It made sense in my head, but I had a feeling it might not hold up once I'd said it out loud. "I just thought – You know, my visions, Mike's sketchbook, finding the cave … That can't all just be random, right?"

"Can't it?"

"Stuff like this doesn't just happen," I said. "There's got to be a reason for it."

Luke was silent for a long time.

"What about Reeve?" he asked, voice low as we approached the front office. "Was there a reason for that too?"

I stared down at the grass, guilt flaring up again.

We were the reason for that one.

"Sorry," said Luke. "Sorry, that was stupid."

We chained up our bikes without speaking and cut across the quad in the direction of the hall.

Thursday morning. Assembly.

"We did get some answers though, right?" said Luke, checking that no one was listening in. "I mean, we know that whoever's handing out orders to Peter's mates is serious enough to brand them all with those tattoos."

"You should've seen the look on Mike's face when they got them. He was so –" I hesitated, struggling to put words to that crazed gleam I'd seen in Mike's eye. "It was – Whatever this thing is, he *believes* in it. He's committed, one hundred percent. He said it was their *destiny.*"

"Destiny," Luke repeated. "Right."

I thought again of the people in the white robes. So far, the closest thing we had to a suspect was a drawing in a sketchbook.

"I dunno," I said. "I'm still not sure how any of that helps us, unless their destiny is to get rid of Shackleton for us."

"Doubt it," said Luke, "seeing as Cathryn reckons we're the ones who killed those people in the DVD."

"Why?" I said, suddenly realizing how much this had been bugging me. "Why would she ever think that? It's the most – How on earth does she think we did it?"

"Dunno, but we've probably missed our chance to ask," said Luke. "After yesterday, I don't think they'll be asking Peter to hang out with them anytime soon."

But as we approached the glass doors out in front

of the hall, I realized that might not be such a problem after all.

There was a body pressed up against the other side of the glass, standing in the little foyer area between the front doors and the hall itself.

Peter's body.

Cathryn had him pinned to the wall, her face centimeters from his.

What now? I thought, getting ready to go to his rescue.

Then I saw the expression on Cathryn's face.

Oh.

She leaned forward, brought her hands up to his neck, and kissed him.

Peter's eyes went wide, but he didn't try to fight her. He waved his hands around for a minute, like he didn't know what to do with them, then finally brought them to rest on her hips.

I felt a tiny glimmer of relief – like, for half a second, a giant weight had been lifted off me – but then the logical part of my brain kicked in and the weight came plummeting back down again.

"What is he *doing?*" Luke whispered.

"What does it look like?" I said, flaring up.

He was doing what any guy like Peter does when a girl who looks like Cathryn makes a move on him: shrugging his shoulders and letting it happen.

"But she thinks he's a killer!" said Luke.

"Who cares?" I hissed, striding towards the nearest open doorway. "The point is she's dangerous, and we can't afford to have Peter –"

Luke latched on to my wrist.

"Not now," he said.

"Well how long do you think they're going to need?" I snapped.

"If we go in there now, he'll just overreact and blow up at us, and we'll end up in Pryor's office," said Luke. He started towards the other end of the hall. "C'mon, come inside and we can sort him out later."

I looked back at Peter and Cathryn. Still going. They'd attracted a little crowd of Year 7s, but it didn't seem like either of them had noticed.

A hundred girls in this school and you pick the one with the mass-murdering mum.

I bit my tongue and followed Luke, heading inside through the doors at the far end.

We'd barely made it into the hall when I heard Peter's voice behind me.

"Jordan! Jordan, wait!" He came racing in from the foyer, wiping his mouth with the back of his hand.

My teeth clenched. "What?"

"It wasn't me!" he said. "I was – I just found her and I was trying to get her to tell me about yesterday and – and then she pushed me up against the wall and she …"

"Yeah. We saw."

"Jordan, please, you know I'm – That wasn't anything!"

"Come on," I said. "Let's find somewhere to sit."

I walked down to the front of the hall, and picked out some seats right in the middle. No point trying to be inconspicuous anymore.

Luke sat down next to me, leaving Peter stranded on the far side. He sent me a pained look.

Then his face brightened.

He jumped up in his seat and leaned across Luke to look at me. "What if it's Bill?"

"What if *what's* Bill?" said Luke, pushing him off.

"What if he's the one who's been telling my old

154

mates what to do all this time?"

"How?" said Luke. "The Co-operative has him. They've had him locked up since forever."

"Yeah," said Peter, excitedly. "Yeah, exactly. Remember what he said when they were chasing him down in the tunnels? *'Find me under the ground!'*"

"So?" said Luke.

"What if they've still got him down there somewhere?" Peter answered. "That's how he's communicating with Mike and the others through the locker. He's sending them instructions to help get him out!"

He kept glancing over at me like he was hoping this amazing insight would convince me to forgive him.

"Still doesn't explain the cave," said Luke. "Besides, wasn't that cage or whatever that your dad built supposed to stop –?"

Luke didn't finish his sentence. The crowd around us was quickly going quiet, drawn to the sound of booming footsteps echoing up from the stage. It wasn't Pryor. But it wasn't Stapleton either.

It was Doctor Montag.

He crossed to the lectern at the front of the

stage, looking slightly harried, and leaned in to the microphone. "Mrs. Stapleton will be here shortly to continue with your usual assembly, but I've asked for just a few minutes of your time to make you aware of an important new initiative of Phoenix Medical's healthcare program."

We were sitting right in front of him, but he seemed to be carefully avoiding looking at us.

"As you know," Montag continued, "we at the medical center are dedicated to providing the people of Phoenix with the highest possible standard of care. As the needs of this town change, we need to ensure that our healthcare practices continue to stay one step ahead."

A chill raced up my back.

Those *changing needs* better not have had anything to do with Georgia or the baby.

"Tomorrow morning, here at school, my medical staff and I will be carrying out compulsory blood testing of all Phoenix High students, as part of a town-wide screening program."

A torrent of whispers filled the hall. Montag raised his voice to silence them.

"This testing is being conducted for your own safety and well-being." His eyes still slid over us like we weren't there, but there was no mistaking the warning in his voice. "Your cooperation is appreciated."

He turned from the lectern and left the stage without another word.

The house was quiet when I got back from school. I dropped my bag off in my room, thinking I was the only one home, then went downstairs for something to eat and found Mum in the family room, lying on the couch with her hands on her stomach. The baby had grown heaps, even in the last week, and the bump under Mum's hands was becoming extremely noticeable.

She glanced up as I walked in. Her face was fixed with the worn-out look that she seemed to carry with her all the time these days. She'd been crying.

"Come here," she said.

"What's wrong?"

She waved me over impatiently. "Just –"

I bent down next to her. She grabbed my hand and pressed it to her stomach.

"Are you serious?" I said. "It's already –?"

Something bumped the palm of my hand.

"There!" said Mum. "Feel that?"

Another bump, and it was like a scalpel straight through my chest. A tear rolled down my cheek and I didn't try to stop it. For a second, everything else just disappeared and all I could feel was that tiny body reaching out to push against mine.

"Kicking," said Mum, head falling back to her pillow. "Seven weeks and he's already kicking."

"He?" I said, snapping out of it.

Mum shrugged. "Just guessing."

I stood up. "Where's Georgia? She needs to feel –"

Mum's smile disappeared.

"She's back at the medical center. The blood test Dr. Montag took on Tuesday turned up something –"

"Blood test?"

"Yeah," said Mum, trying to hide the concern in her voice. "He didn't really explain why he took it, but – Anyway, he wants to keep her overnight, just to make sure everything's okay."

It might have been the worst panic I'd felt since we'd gotten here. Something in Georgia's blood. Something serious enough to make Montag start screening the whole town.

"Then what are you doing?" I demanded. "Why aren't you down there? Who's with her?"

"Jordan – Calm down," said Mum, sitting up. "You think we'd leave her in that place by herself? Dad's with her. He's going to stay there tonight." She gave a halfhearted smile. "He said I'd seen more than my fair share of that place."

"Oh."

They wouldn't do anything to Georgia. Not with Dad there.

Mum got to her feet and gave me a hug. Her stomach pressed into mine and I felt the baby move again.

"We're going home," she said.

I pulled back. "What?"

"Dad and I have been talking about it. Phoenix just isn't working out for us. As soon as we can organize a flight, we're heading back to Brisbane. You can go back to your old school and –"

Mum frowned at the look on my face.

I knew what she and Dad were like when they fixed their minds on something – and I knew the kind of fight they'd put up when Ketterley told them there were "no flights available." Trying to leave Phoenix wasn't just impossible. It was dangerous.

"I thought I could handle it," said Mum, voice starting to crack. "When we first found out – I thought I could handle having the baby out here away from my sisters, but …"

I pulled her in closer again, hugging her tight.

Lost for words.

"We'll work it out," I said eventually, knowing how meaningless it sounded. "We'll figure something out."

Mum sniffed and nodded. "We will."

The tears were coming again. I went back upstairs, holding them off just long enough to get up to my room. I collapsed on my bed, staring at the ceiling, losing it completely, angry and scared and trapped in a world too big and too dark to even wrap my head around.

I thought about going over to Luke's.

No. He had enough to deal with without me showing up on his doorstep, crying. Besides, I didn't trust myself not to do anything stupid if Montag was over there again.

I decided to email him instead. I sat up, coughing, and pulled out my laptop.

Something else came out with it.

A brown paper lunch bag, folded in half.

And even before I opened it, I knew there'd be some new nightmare waiting inside.

JORDAN,
MEET ME BEHIND THE SCHOOL HALL
AT 6 P.M. TONIGHT.
COME ALONE.

Chapter 15

At 5:45 p.m., I poked my head into the kitchen. "Back in a bit."

"Where are you going?" Mum asked. "Dinner's nearly ready."

"It's school-related," I said, which was technically true.

Mum looked out the window. It was already starting to get dark.

"I'll be really quick," I said, which was probably less true.

Mum didn't look happy, but she seemed too exhausted to argue. "All right. Just make sure you're back before curfew. That Officer Calvin is a madman."

I stopped on the veranda and decided to take my bike down with me. Easier to make a quick getaway if I needed to.

Not that I was the only one out here. There were still plenty of people out watering their gardens or walking their pets. But I had a feeling none of their hearts were hammering quite as hard as mine was right now.

What was I about to walk in on?

My first thought was Mike, Cathryn and Tank. I'd had classes with all of them today. They would've had plenty of opportunity to slip a note in my bag. But why would they want to talk to just me? Why not all three of us?

What if it was worse than that? What if they'd delivered that message on behalf of whoever they were answering to? Overseers? Was that what Mike had called them?

I shivered.

Why? What was it about those stupid drawings that bothered me so much? Didn't I have enough *real* danger in my life?

The back gate was locked by the time I got to

school. A good sign. Hopefully, it meant everyone was out of there. I jumped the fence and hauled my bike over after me.

I checked my watch.

5:52 p.m.

Enough time to take the long way around and hopefully come up on whoever this was from behind. I walked my bike across the lawn, keeping an eye out for security.

The school had been a pretty smart choice. The guards still came through here, but they were nowhere near as –

Oh no. No. Not now.

I stumbled, gagging, the worst pain so far.

Another vision.

Why couldn't they ever happen when I was home in bed?

Everything spun. The grass turned to sludge under my feet. I searched frantically for a place to hide, not wanting anyone to see me while I was out. There was some landscaping a couple of meters away. I staggered over, hauling my bike, and collapsed down into the bushes.

And then the bushes disappeared.

Night flashed into day.

Rough, rocky ground under me.

The nausea faded and I stretched back up onto my hands and knees. My eyes swung into focus. And suddenly, I was a completely different kind of disoriented.

Phoenix had vanished.

The whole town, gone.

And the bush had evaporated with it.

Nothing but dry, barren wasteland in every direction. The same kind of terrain we'd seen when we tried to escape over the wall.

I stood up, brushing the dust off my knees. This was different. I wasn't just looking at another time. I was looking at another place.

But…

No. That wasn't right. The slope of the ground was still the same. And now that I was looking for them, I was pretty sure I could pick out all the places where the buildings on the main street should be.

I was still here.

So when was this? Was I back before the town

was built? Or was this a glimpse of the future, of what the Co-operative was planning to do to with Phoenix after –

After Tabitha.

I turned around, eyes passing over the place where my house had stood until about thirty seconds ago. The wasteland and sky shifted at my movement, like ripples spreading out across a pond.

There was something out there.

A concrete building. Square and gray, like a prison or something. The building was maybe two stories tall, although it was hard to tell from this far away. It stood a little way out into the bush at the north end of town. At least, that's where it would have been if the bush and the town still existed.

There was a dark shape painted on the side of the building – a logo or something, almost as big as the building itself – but I couldn't make out what it was. The landscape was still shimmering around me, too unstable to catch the details on something so far off.

Stop moving, I reminded myself. *You're making it worse.*

I held my body as still as possible, squinting out at the concrete box. Slowly, the world began to settle down and, for a fraction of a second, I got a clear glimpse of the shape.

A black spiral.

And then it was over. The sky caved in and the land rolled up into nothing and I dropped to my knees with the violent urge to throw up.

Down into the flower bed. I gagged a couple of times, fists clenching handfuls of soil, temporarily blinded by the sudden change in light. The sun was setting again.

I got up, dragging my bike back onto the grass.

The nerves came back and I felt myself sweating despite the cold. I still had a meeting to get to.

I rolled the bike up onto the concrete, taking the narrow path that led between the hall and the aquatic center, looking for escape routes along the way in case this turned nasty.

I froze at the corner. No sound, but there was something flickering in the shadows.

Light from a handful of tiny flames – like the candles in the cave.

They're just people, I thought, bracing myself. *Even if it is the guys in white – They're still only human.*

But what did that even mean anymore?

There was a sharp stone on the ground a few steps away, about as big as my hand. I picked it up, getting ready to defend myself if I had to.

I swung the stone up in front of me, leapt out from around the corner –

And realized I was dealing with something completely different.

"Peter?"

He was sitting cross-legged on the ground with his back to me. He jumped at the sound of my voice, then turned around and grinned. "Surprise!"

"What –?" I dropped the stone. "Hang on. You left that note?"

Slowly, my brain absorbed the scene. There was a picnic blanket spread out in front of him, ringed with candles, and covered in food and drink.

Food and drink for two people.

"Jordan," he said, getting up. "This morning with Cat – It was stupid, okay? I don't know why – But seriously, Jordan, she's not – She isn't anything."

I glanced from the picnic to Peter and back again, nervous energy shifting into anger. "That's what this is about?"

"I wanted to make it up to you," said Peter.

"So, what, you thought you'd leave me a note with no name on it? Freak me out completely? Drag me into the school right before curfew?"

"No!" said Peter, getting up. "Jordan, no, that's not – This was supposed to be –"

"Yeah, it's pretty obvious what this was supposed to be," I said, turning my bike around. "Not interested."

"Jordan!"

"You know Shackleton is watching us!" I shouted. "You know how dangerous this all is! Why would you ever think this was a good idea?"

Peter swayed like I'd just punched him.

I climbed onto my bike, knowing I was only going to get angrier at him the longer I stayed here.

He grabbed the handlebars. "Jordan, stop."

"Peter, seriously, just –"

"I love you."

I took my feet back off the pedals.

"Why?" I said. "Why are you doing this?"

He put his hands on mine. "Jordan, I –"

"You don't," I said, pulling free. "Okay? You don't. That's not what this is."

Peter pushed away from the bike, flaring up.

"No? What is it, then?"

I didn't answer.

"Come on, Jordan," said Peter, voice rising. "Tell me. Please. What am I *really* feeling?"

"We should get out of here," I said.

"Why?" snapped Peter. "So you can go over to bloody *Luke's* and tell him –"

"Stop it," I said. "Just stop being a child for two seconds and think about where we are! It'll be dark in like ten minutes. After what happened yesterday, do you really want –?"

"Hey – you two!"

Right on cue, a pair of security officers had just stepped out from around the corner.

Peter swore, and started running.

"What a surprise," I muttered.

I turned my bike around again and pedaled away across the grass.

Chapter 16

"So what do you think this is?" Luke asked, as we lined up outside the gym for Dr. Montag's blood screening. "What do you reckon they're testing us for?"

I didn't want to think about it. Georgia was still stuck at the medical center, and whatever this blood thing was, it had all started with her freakout at the mall. And the more I thought about it, the more likely it seemed that Luke was right, that all of this stuff was connected – and that Shackleton knew it.

Which would explain the blood tests. The Co-operative would want to know who else was … *changing*, so they could deal with us before we all turned into Crazy Bills.

"I dunno," I said, finally answering Luke's question. "I reckon we'll find out soon enough, though."

Peter just grunted. He'd barely spoken all day. I felt kind of bad about the way I'd torn shreds off him last night, but I still wasn't ready to forgive his stupidity just yet.

Thankfully, the security guards had given up the chase almost right away, once they realized we were leaving the school grounds – which meant they'd probably just found us by accident, rather than being sent after us by Shackleton.

Either way, trying to apologize to Peter would mean bringing up last night again, and I really didn't see that going well.

The line moved up a bit, far enough for me to see inside the gym. Montag and a couple of nurses were set up in little booths in the middle of the hall. Each booth had a stool, a table covered with what I guessed was blood testing equipment, and a curtain that got pulled across the front while Montag and the nurses did whatever they did.

Every now and then, there was a little yelp of pain

from behind one of the curtains.

"I *hate* needles," Luke whispered.

The line moved again, and I nudged him forward. "Probably not going to be the worst one we've had since we got here."

We walked through the door. Mr. Hanger was prowling around, supervising. He must have caught the bitter look on Peter's face, because he stopped on his way past.

"Is there a problem, Peter?"

"No, sir."

It looked like it was taking all of Peter's self-control not to lash out at him.

Mr. Hanger considered him for a minute, then continued down the line.

I saw Jeremy, the kid who'd given me the handprint, standing up at the front. I wanted to go over and warn him to get out of there. But what was the point? If the Co-operative really wanted his blood, they'd have no problem going to his house and getting it.

I watched Jeremy step into the booth. The curtain closed, and it occurred to me that things could go downhill for him even quicker if his skin imprinted on the nurse's hands. But before long, the booth opened again and Jeremy walked away, rubbing his arm.

A few minutes later, we were at the front of the line.

"Next –" said Montag, pushing his curtain aside. "Oh." He waved me over to the booth.

"Roll up your sleeve, please," he said in his doctor voice as I sat down.

As soon as the curtain was closed, I jumped back up. *What are you doing to my sister?*

Montag looked down at me, expressionless, like I wasn't even worth reacting to.

"Roll up your sleeve, please."

I didn't move.

"Do you think you will put her in less danger with this behavior?" Montag asked.

I sat down and rolled up my sleeve.

"Stretch out your arm."

Montag picked up a black rubber ring thing and slipped it over my left hand, up to my forearm. He pumped it up until it was crushing in on my arm.

"She's six years old," I said. "You're a doctor. You really have no problem with any of this?"

He handed me a yellow stress ball with a smiley face on it. "Squeeze that for me."

I crushed the ball, and the veins on my arm started to swell.

"Very good," he said, raising a syringe into the air. "Hold still."

I flinched as the needle dug into my arm. "Déjà vu, eh, doc?"

A flicker of discomfort in his eyes. He finished drawing out the blood and replaced the needle with a cotton ball. I held it to the puncture mark on my arm.

"What's the matter, doc?" I whispered, trying to keep my voice steady. "Don't want to think about it? You going to pretend it was someone else holding me down over that table? Lifting up my shirt? *Injecting* me? That was only three kids, doc. If you can't handle that, what are you going to do when Tabitha —"

"You can take that away now," said Montag, holding out a band-aid to replace the cotton ball.

"Ah, but you don't actually have to see that happen, do you, doc? You don't have to watch *those* kids twisting on the ground. You can just hide out in that bunker of yours and pretend –"

Too far.

There was a clatter of equipment and suddenly Montag was latching on to my collar with both hands.

"Let go of me," I spat.

"Listen, you ignorant child," Montag breathed into my ear, "if you had any idea –"

And then I did something *really* stupid.

Not thinking about anything other than getting free, I flung out my arm and grabbed a handful of curtain, yanking it down hard towards me. The curtain tore, billowing down to the ground, and suddenly there was nothing separating Montag and me from the whole crowd of students waiting outside.

Shouts across the gym.

Montag recoiled, almost crashing into the table behind him in his hurry to get off me.

"Jordan Burke!" roared Mr. Hanger, storming over.

Peter was still waiting at the front of the line. He rushed over, and the kids behind him followed, crowding in for a closer look.

"What is going on here?" Mr. Hanger demanded.

"What does it look like, sir?" said Peter. "He was –"

"I didn't ask you to speak, Weir," said Hanger.

Luke burst out of the next booth, his nurse trailing after him.

"This young lady just tried to attack me," said Montag, quickly regaining his composure.

"She did not, sir!" said Peter. "It was him!"

A few noises of agreement from the crowd.

"Enough," Mr. Hanger shouted.

"With your permission," said Montag, "I'd like to escort Miss Burke to the principal's office."

"Sir!" Peter protested.

Mr. Hanger sneered at Peter, then grabbed me by the arm. "No need. I'll take her."

Luke opened his mouth, but I glared at him to shut up. They wouldn't do anything to me. Not now. Not after a bunch of kids had just seen Dr. Montag's hands at my throat.

But then Peter stepped up to Mr. Hanger, right in his face. "Let go."

"I'm warning you, Mr. Weir –"

"LET GO OF HER!"

Mr. Hanger turned away from him, leading me towards the door. The crowd parted to let us through.

There was a strangled shout and suddenly I was yanked sideways. A jolt of pain tore through my shoulder as Mr. Hanger went flying, still holding my arm. He crumpled to the floor and I finally pulled free.

I got halfway to my feet and stopped. Peter was sprawled on Mr. Hanger's back, face spewing over with rage. He clawed at Hanger's neck, grabbing it from behind, dragging his head up from the floor.

A nurse ran forward. "Hey, kid, come on –"

"Peter!" yelled Luke. "What are you doing?"

With a savage scream, he slammed Mr. Hanger's head back down into the ground. There was a horrible cracking sound and Hanger howled with pain. He lifted his head, blood streaming from his nose.

More gasps from the crowd. Luke backed away, looking sick.

As a teacher, Mr. Hanger was intimidating. But he wasn't young, and he wasn't strong. He shouted and kicked, but it got him nowhere.

My mind screamed, but it was like I'd forgotten how to talk.

Montag raced up and grabbed Peter around the middle. Peter held on tight to Hanger's throat, shouting out again, mindless and frantic. His head caught Montag in the chin.

Stop! No, no, no, Peter, please –

The doc fell back, losing his grip, and Peter smashed Mr. Hanger's face to the floor again.

"Peter!" I screamed, finding my voice. "Stop!"

But Peter seemed beyond hearing. He was all instinct, all animal rage.

"Please ..." Mr. Hanger moaned. "Please, I'm sorry ..."

Montag and the nurse leapt forward together, grabbing Peter around the shoulders. Peter's fingernails dug into Hanger's skin, drawing blood as he fought to keep his grip.

I charged forward, dropping to my hands and knees in front of Peter's face.

"STOP!" I screamed. "Peter, stop!"

Peter yelled out again, tears of rage streaming from his eyes.

And finally, he stopped.

His fingers slowly drew back from around Mr.

Hanger's neck.

Montag and the nurse hauled Peter to his feet. He looked at me, dazed, then down at his bloodied hands. Hanger lay there under him, taking deep, shuddering breaths.

"They were going to hurt you," Peter said.

"They still might," hissed a voice from behind us. Pryor.

Chapter 17

Peter shrugged off Montag and the nurse, stumbling over Mr. Hanger's collapsed body. His face was white, the reality of what he'd just done starting to sink in.

Pryor looked to Montag. "Get Noah," she said in an undertone, inclining her head at one of the blood testing booths that still had a curtain across it.

Montag nodded and slipped inside, hand in his pocket. Pulling out his phone to call Shackleton. One of only ten phones in Phoenix that actually worked.

I got up. My hands were sticky with Mr. Hanger's blood. I wiped them off on my skirt.

The two nurses swooped down on Hanger, armed with a first aid kit. They rolled him onto his back, drawing even more noises of shock from the crowd. His face was a bloodied mess. Mr. Hanger was the most hated teacher in the school, and I was sure plenty of these kids had fantasized about taking a swing at him. But the reality was something completely different.

"All of you – out!" shouted Pryor, scattering them. She glanced down at Mr. Hanger. "How is he?"

"He'll live," said one of the nurses, "but –"

"Good." Pryor's attention flashed to Peter, Luke and me. "This way."

She led us out of the gym and across the field to her office.

"Sorry …" Peter mumbled, dazed. "I … I didn't …"

I looked out at the town center, my mind grasping for an escape plan. But running was pointless. One touch of a button and Shackleton could take our legs out from under us.

How had this gotten out of hand so quickly?

Mrs. Stapleton was coming out of the front office as we approached. She froze halfway down the steps, eyes wide at Peter's stained hands and spattered clothes. "Melinda –"

"There's been an incident in the gym," said Pryor. "Take care of it, please." She brushed past Mrs. Stapleton and took us inside.

Before we'd even made it to the giant steel door guarding Pryor's office, Dr. Montag strode into the building behind us.

"Well?" said Pryor, swiping her key card.

"He's coming."

Pryor's door clunked open and she ushered Luke, Peter and me inside. The office was the same as always: huge wooden table, rug on the floor, identical vases of flowers sitting on identical pedestals.

Pryor heaved the door closed behind her, then bent down and rolled the rug up towards her desk, exposing the rough gray tiles underneath.

"Shouldn't be long now," Pryor said, her menacing veneer slipping just slightly.

She was nervous. We'd already stolen her phone and used it to contact Luke's dad on the outside. And now, a whole new mess had just arrived on her turf.

Shackleton had to be losing patience.

By the look of things, Montag wasn't too excited to be here either.

Good.

Still, they both had a whole lot more chance of walking away from this meeting than we did.

A sharp hiss of air cut through the silence, making me jump, and a section of the gray tiles began slowly sinking down into the floor. It dropped about five centimeters, then slid away to the side, revealing a brightly-lit tunnel and a set of silver stairs.

It was a sign of how far we'd all come that they weren't bothering to hide this from us.

I heard gentle padding footsteps, and the withered form of Noah Shackleton came up through the floor to join us.

"Good morning, everyone!" he said brightly, imitating the singsong voice of a kindergarten teacher. He looked around, as though waiting for us all to respond, but the only sound was the tunnel hissing shut at his feet.

Shackleton crossed the newly-restored floor, stopping toe-to-toe with Peter. I tensed, ready to jump in and defend him if I had to.

A grin crept over Shackleton's face as he examined Peter's bloodied clothes. "Dr. Montag tells me you were involved in a dispute with one of your teachers just now."

Peter didn't even look at him.

"Not speaking?" said Shackleton. He pulled out a handkerchief and offered it to Peter. "Here. Why don't you clean yourself up a bit?"

Peter stared at Shackleton's outstretched hand. He glanced over at me, lost. Then he took the handkerchief and slowly began wiping the worst of the blood out from between his fingers.

I watched, skin crawling.

Pryor was looking impatient, but she knew better than to try to hurry things along.

Finally, Peter balled up the handkerchief and let his hands drop by his sides.

Shackleton smiled. "Isn't that better?"

"Sir –" said Pryor, but Shackleton held up a hand.

"Now then," he said to Peter. "Would you care to remind me of the agreement we made a fortnight ago when you and your friends last visited my offices?"

A long silence. Then, still not looking up, Peter said, "You told us … not to tell anyone what we knew … and not to do anything to … not to do anything to make people suspicious."

"I believe my precise words were, *spend the next seventy days quietly attending to your schoolwork and do not put one foot out of line*," said Shackleton in a tone like he was giving Peter half-credit on a math question. "But yes, I believe you've grasped the gist of it."

I closed my eyes, holding down the crippling dread, trying to come up with something to swing things back into our favor.

"However," Shackleton continued, "given that your principal does not usually call upon me to intervene in matters of school discipline – especially those which reflect so poorly on her capacity to maintain order –" he added pointedly, "I can only assume that Ms. Pryor is of the opinion that you have now violated our agreement. I trust you recall the consequences of such a violation?"

Peter nodded.

"You do," said Shackleton. "In that case, your actions today would seem particularly foolhardy – especially given that your friend Jordan's younger sister is currently in our custody at the medical center. It would be only too easy for something unfortunate –"

"You stay away from her!" I said.

"Jordan," said Shackleton, turning, "you are in a poor position to be making demands."

"Ask Dr. Montag what started all this!" I said desperately. "Ask him why Peter blew up at Mr. Hanger."

Shackleton reeled back, a caricature of shock. He raised an eyebrow at Dr. Montag. "Rob?"

"Sir," said Montag, "Peter's reaction was completely disproportionate to any –"

"He attacked me in the blood test booth!" I said, swinging a hand out at Montag.

"Is this true?" asked Shackleton.

Luke opened his mouth to speak, but Peter jumped in first.

"Of course it's bloody true," he said, firing up again. "Ask the fifty kids who saw it happen!"

No fake surprise this time. Shackleton rounded on Montag. "How much of a problem is this going to be?"

"The students only saw a fraction of it," the doctor said hurriedly. "A few seconds at most."

"And the beating of the teacher?"

"They saw the whole thing, but Melinda sent them out as soon as she arrived."

"Good," said Shackleton. "Contact Brian as soon as we're finished here. I want the write-up ready for this afternoon's *Herald*. Two known delinquents refuse to take part in blood testing, become violent, attack teaching staff and medical personnel. Despite everyone's best efforts, the incident ends in tragedy."

I thought *tragedy* was a bit strong. What Peter had done to Mr. Hanger was horrific, but the nurse had said he'd be okay.

"I want quotes from anonymous students and a nice, close photograph of the injured staff member," Shackleton said. "Let them see the damage. Give me a shot of Peter, too."

Montag nodded. "Front page?"

"Absolutely," said Shackleton. "And Rob, please ensure Brian understands the importance of making the *correct* version of events available to the public."

"Yeah, right," said Peter. "As if people are going to believe —"

"I think you'll find that people will believe what we tell them to believe," said Shackleton, reaching into his suit pocket. "Especially under the circumstances."

"What circumstances?" asked Peter.

Shackleton put a finger to his lips and pulled out his phone. He went around behind Pryor's desk and sat back in her chair with the phone held up to his ear.

I started towards the desk. If he did anything to my sister –

"I wouldn't," Montag warned.

Shackleton's eyes lit up. "Tori, how are you? … No. No, it was nothing serious. Just some trouble down at the school …"

Shackleton chuckled. "No, nothing like that … I assume we're still on for dinner this evening? … Lovely. Listen, Tori, would you mind stepping into my office for a moment? I need you to activate Peter Weir's suppressor for me."

He said it so casually that it took me a second to even process it.

And then I snapped, bolting across the tiles, almost tripping over the rolled-up rug.

"No!"

Montag grabbed me from behind.

Peter was quicker. He dived across Pryor's desk. Shackleton rolled back in his chair, still talking into the phone. "Yes – quick as you can please, Tori."

A second later, the phone went clattering across the desk as Peter made another lunge, knocking Shackleton and the chair over backwards.

Montag had his arms bent up under mine, locking my shoulders back against his chest. I jumped up and tucked in my legs, dropping like a rock. Montag lurched forward under the sudden weight, but didn't let go.

"Do you want to be next?" he hissed. "I'm sure Mr. Shackleton could arrange it."

Pryor and Luke were both at the desk by now, staring down from opposite ends. But before either of them had the chance to do anything, Peter had dragged Shackleton up by his jacket and shoved him down on top of the desk.

"CALL HER BACK!" he shouted, high-pitched with desperation. "Call her back and tell her not to do it!"

Shackleton coughed. "I'm afraid it's too late for that."

"No! You *call her off!*" Tears were pouring down Peter's face. He snatched the phone off the table and slapped it into the side of Shackleton's head. "You

CALL her! I won't spend the rest of my life in a freaking –"

Peter's pleading turned into a deafening, wordless scream as the suppressor kicked in. He stumbled, teeth clenched, eyes closed, then cried out again and fell to the ground behind Pryor's desk.

Shackleton got up, massaging his back, and said, "I really am sorry."

Luke reached down to help, then recoiled as Peter batted him away.

Peter grabbed Pryor's desk with both hands. He launched himself at Shackleton, spewing obscenities, raging and begging until it was all drowned out in another gut-wrenching scream.

Montag's grip on me began to loosen, and I finally kicked my way free of him. But it was already over. Nothing to do but stand and watch.

Peter staggered back, out into the middle of the room, legs failing again. I swept forward and caught him around the waist, holding him up.

"The pain will be over soon," said Shackleton, smoothing down his hair. "Fifteen minutes and you won't feel a thing."

Peter stopped shouting to take a breath, and I heard the bell ringing out on the playground.

"My goodness," said Shackleton, eyes flitting between Luke and me. "Recess already. I suppose you two had better be off."

"If you think we're just going to leave him here with you –"

"I believe you know what your alternative is," said Shackleton, bending down to retrieve his phone.

Dr. Montag reached out to take Peter.

Peter looked up at me, eyes unfocused, full of fear. "Jordan …"

But staying here and getting paralyzed too wasn't going to help him.

I stared at the doc, looking for some trace of humanity.

Nothing.

"You bastard," I breathed, hefting Peter into his arms.

Pryor pulled her office door open a crack, looked both ways along the corridor, then ushered the two of us outside.

Chapter 18

"Despite the best efforts of teaching staff and medical center personnel to restrain the student, the incident continued to escalate until, while attempting to resist capture, Weir fell from a piece of gym apparatus, sustaining serious back injuries. The youth is currently being treated in Phoenix Medical, but doctors fear that the damage to his spinal column may be irreparable."

Luke threw down the newspaper.

We were sitting outside Flameburger, watching the doors to the medical center. As soon as school finished, we'd tried to get in to see Peter. But, of course, Montag had left orders for us not to be allowed in.

My elbows dug into the table, hands nursing my

throbbing head. I'd spent the whole day just trying to hold myself together, avoiding the stream of kids hammering me for every gory detail of the attack.

Even now, they were staring over from the other tables. I could hear them whispering, daring each other to come over and talk to me. I'd never seen so many of them reading the newspaper.

It was just like Shackleton had predicted. Even the kids who had seen it all happen seemed to be swallowing the *Herald*'s version of the story. They'd all been so well-trained to think the worst of us that they were more than willing to believe Peter had brought his injuries upon himself. To believe I was some doctor-attacking psychopath.

"They saw him stand up," said Luke, eyes down on the pile of chips in front of him. "He let go of Hanger and he stood up."

"Yeah, but then Pryor sent them all out," I said. "Anything could have happened after that."

The problem was, Shackleton's story kind of made sense. It was reality that was hard to swallow.

I gazed back over at the medical center, barely seeing it. I could feel the tears coming again.

We'd left him. We'd left him behind and let Shackleton take him away.

"We had a fight last night," I said.

Luke looked up. "You and Peter?"

"He left me a note. Wanted me to meet him out behind the school. But he didn't tell me it was him. So I went out there and ..."

I hesitated. Somehow it didn't feel right to tell Luke the whole story.

"I overreacted," I said. "He blew up. And then security chased us off before we could talk about any of it. And then he came to school all angry, and –"

Luke stared across the table at me. "This isn't your fault, Jordan."

"Who tore down that curtain?" I said. "Who was Peter trying to protect when he –?"

"When he smashed Hanger's face in?" said Luke. "Jordan, this didn't happen because you ripped a curtain. What Peter did today, that wasn't normal anger. This has been coming for a while."

I put my head back down in my hands. "We need to get him out of there," I said.

"They'll let him out eventually," said Luke. "They

just need to keep him long enough to back up their story." He glanced over at the medical center. "Uh-oh."

Officer Calvin was walking up the steps.

He didn't look happy.

Then again, Calvin pretty much never looked happy unless he was pointing a gun at someone.

For about five seconds, I wondered what he was up to. Then the medical center doors slid open and I lost interest completely. Dad had just walked out, carrying Georgia on his back. He brushed past Calvin and continued down the stairs.

"I'll email you," I said, leaving Luke at the table.

I was over there almost before Dad's foot left the bottom step, doing my best to look like I hadn't just been through a trauma.

"Jordan!" said Georgia, swinging down off Dad's back for a hug.

"Hey, Georgia," I said. "How was the hospital?"

"*Boring*," she said heavily, rolling her eyes.

It was the best answer I could have asked for. Warmth surged back into my body – then retreated again as I saw the look on Dad's face.

"Everything okay?" I asked.

"Hard to say," he muttered, starting towards home. "They told us she's fine. But that's about all they told us. What about you? The nurses were talking about a fight at the school. I saw one of your teachers come in with a broken nose."

"Guess what," said Georgia.

"Mr. Hanger," I said. "Yeah, he was – He got beat up pretty bad."

Then, thinking it was better for him to hear it from me: "Did they tell you I was involved? That I was refusing to take the blood test?"

"Yes, they did," said Dad slowly. "But that's not what really happened, is it?"

My head started pounding again. "What?"

"Jordan, if you didn't take the blood test, then why do you have that bandage on your arm?"

I gaped at him, grasping for an explanation, but it was like there was a drum beating in my brain.

"Guess what," said Georgia again.

"Why do you keep taking the blame for all this?" Dad pressed. "If you're doing this to keep someone else out of trouble …"

"No – I'm not – I was just …" I trailed off, wishing Luke and I had spent more time getting our story worked out.

"I don't know where the *Herald* is getting its information, but it's time someone set them straight."

"No – Dad, it's okay," I said, ignoring the sudden temperature drop in my insides. "It doesn't bother me. I mean, as long as you and Mum know it's not true, why would I care?"

"It bothers me," said Dad. "Someone's getting away with this stuff at your expense. It isn't right."

"Dad, seriously, it's not a big deal."

"Jordan!" shouted Georgia. "I said, *guess what!*"

"What?" I said.

"We're going home to Brisbane!"

Dad looked at me. "I assume Mum's talked to you?"

"Yeah," I said, grateful for the interruption. "Have you booked a flight yet?"

"Hopefully," said Dad. "Mum was going to sort it out this morning."

Which means she's argued with every possible person by now, I thought. *And been knocked back by all of them.*

We turned off at the park and headed up the

street to our house.

"What about Max?" said Georgia.

"You can send him postcards from Brisbane," said Dad. "And he can come and visit anytime he wants."

"What about Luke?"

"Luke?" said Dad. "Jordan's friend Luke?"

"Yeah. If we move away, then how will they get married?"

She stared at up at me, grinning wildly.

Dad raised an eyebrow. "We'll cross that bridge when we come to it."

Our house came into view and Georgia wriggled down from my arms, running the rest of the way to the front door. By the time Dad and I caught up, the door was already open and she was pressing her hands against Mum's stomach.

"Whoa, Mum," she said. "Your baby is getting so fat!"

"How is she?" Mum asked. "Anything new?"

"Not since my email," said Dad.

"Hey, baby, I hope you don't get *too* fat," said Georgia, speaking into Mum's bellybutton. "You might squash yourself!"

"Seems normal to me," said Mum. She smiled and turned back into the house.

"Did you book the flights?" asked Dad, following.

Mum groaned. "I tried everything. I even tracked down Aaron Ketterley in town! Apparently, they're booked solid."

"For how long?"

"I don't know. Indefinitely." Mum dropped onto the couch. "Which doesn't even make sense. Think about it: who's left Phoenix since we got here?"

Dad thought. "There were those two security guards who left a couple of weeks ago."

"And?"

"And … I don't know."

"We've only been here a couple of months," I said, really not liking the direction this conversation was headed.

"There must be something else wrong," said Mum. "A technical problem they don't want to tell us about."

"Does the baby need a ticket?" asked Georgia.

"No, sweetheart," said Mum. "The baby gets to ride with me."

"And will Grandma and Grandpa come to the airport again?"

Mum pulled her in for a hug. "I'm not sure, Georgia. We'll see."

"I'm going to go and see Ketterley in the morning," said Dad. "Sort this out."

"Dad –" I said, hating to think what might happen if they pushed this. "Why don't you just wait? I mean, we can stick it out here for a bit longer, can't we?"

Mum looked at me like she was seeing something for the first time. "Jordan …" she said slowly. "Do you know something we don't?"

"No!" I said. "What would I –? I just think we should be careful. I mean, if they are covering something up about the flights …"

Dad put an arm around me.

"I'll be careful," he promised. "But I won't let my family be bullied."

I put my head on his shoulder, wishing there was some way to tell him just how big these bullies were.

This was bad.

What if Ketterley thought Dad knew too much?

What if he thought I'd told him?

No. I wouldn't. I would never put them in danger, and Shackleton knew it.

He had to.

I collapsed back against the tree, watching the people sitting in cafés all along the side of the mall, enjoying their Saturday like there was nothing wrong in the world.

Why couldn't my parents be like that?

Dad'll be fine, I told myself. *He knows how to handle himself.*

I tried to push it aside and think about something else for a while. But every time I closed my eyes, I saw Peter screaming in pain. Or bodies bursting into nothingness. Or white-robed specters coming to suck my brains out.

I wished Luke would hurry up and get here.

I looked over at the playground. Reeve's wife,

Katie, was waiting at the bottom of the slide, hands outstretched to catch her son. We'd seen them playing there before, back when –

Back when there were three of them.

Then someone else ran out from behind the playground. It was Mike. He bolted across the grass, looking frantic, head spinning in all directions.

I pushed myself to my feet, psyching myself up for a chase.

But as soon as I started moving, Mike spotted me. He ran straight over, looking even more panicked than he had when he'd found us in the cave.

"Peter," Mike demanded. "Where is he?"

"They took him to the medical center," I said.

"Don't be stupid. Where is he?"

"Mike, seriously, he's –"

"He's not," said Mike. "Not anymore. Someone's taken him."

Chapter 19

"What?"

"You swear it wasn't you?" said Mike, raking his hair back out of his eyes. "You didn't, like, break him out last night or something?"

I grabbed him with both hands. "What are you talking about? When did this happen?"

"I just came from the medical center," he said, shaking me off. "We went in to see Pete yesterday after school, but they said he wasn't having visitors until this morning. So we go back, and the whole place is in freaking chaos. Pete's parents crying, nurses running in and out, the doc shouting at people to figure out where he's gone …"

I pictured Peter being taken into the medical center, raging and screaming. Shackleton standing over him, smiling. Deciding he was too big a security risk. Phoning in the order to take away more than his legs.

"How long ago was this?" I asked.

"I dunno," said Mike. "Fifteen, twenty minutes?"

I started running.

"Wait," said Mike, chasing after me, "they're not letting anyone in –"

He broke off, focusing on keeping up with me. I dashed along the row of cafés, the too-white walls of the medical center already in my sights.

"Why were you looking for me?" I asked, when it was obvious Mike wasn't going to give up and leave me alone.

"We thought you guys –"

"No, I mean, why do you care?"

I twisted sideways, edging between a café table and a couple of bikes zooming past in the opposite direction.

"He's my – mate," Mike puffed indignantly, still following.

"Sure he is."

I turned left, up the road between the mall and the medical center. The only asphalt road in Phoenix. There was a truck parked at the end of the road. Two guys in white jumped out of the back and I almost had a heart attack.

But they were just delivery guys, bringing in supplies from "out of town."

I threw a glance over my shoulder, checking that Mike hadn't caught my overreaction.

"Look," he said, starting to fall behind now. "We need him, okay?"

I shot past the truck and veered around the corner, onto the main street. I stopped for just a second, scoping out my surroundings. There were two security officers standing at the top of the steps to the medical center, blocking the way inside.

Mike caught up, panting.

"You know what?" he said, catching sight of the guards. "Bad idea."

I ignored him, dashing up the steps two at a time. Mike didn't follow.

One of the guards held out a hand. "Sorry, Miss Burke. Emergency access only."

I recognized the voice. Officer Miller, the guard from the lake.

"It's an emergency," I said, pushing the hand out of the way.

Through the glass, I saw Peter's mum sitting on a waiting room chair, pale and gutted. Peter's dad was parked in his wheelchair, holding her hand. They stared up at a nurse who I thought might have been Mike's mum, and whatever she was telling them, they weren't liking it.

"Miss Burke," said Miller. "If you don't head back downstairs, my orders are to send for Officer Calvin."

I stood my ground, knowing I couldn't let it get that far, but wanting to find out as much as I could before I backed off.

More nurses rushed around inside. No sign of Dr. Montag. The nurse talking to Peter's parents walked away, and Mrs. Weir's head fell to her knees. She shook with tears. Mr. Weir put a hand on her back.

"Miss Burke," said Miller again. "Trust me. You really don't want to mess with the chief right now. Why don't you just head on home?"

I wanted to argue. But even if I did get in there,

what was I planning on doing?

I started back down the steps.

Find Luke, I told myself. *Work this out —*

There was a bang on the other side of the glass doors. I looked back, but from this angle all I could see was a reflection of the security center across the street.

The guards peered through the glass. Miller reached over and unlocked the doors. They slid open.

Mr. Weir glared down at me from the top of the steps. He'd seen me watching him.

I stared back, wondering if I really wanted to have this conversation.

"Excuse me," Mr. Weir muttered, pushing past Miller to the ramp leading down the side of the building.

I faltered for just a second longer, then leapt down the rest of the stairs and went around to meet him at the bottom.

Mike had disappeared. Probably off to find his friends and figure out how something could possibly go wrong in this town without us being behind it.

Peter's dad braked at the bottom of the ramp. He'd grown a beard since the last time we spoke, though it didn't look intentional.

"Please," he said in a ragged whisper. "Tell me where he is."

"We haven't got him!" I said.

"You think I don't know that?" said Mr. Weir. "Fell from a piece of gym apparatus, my arse. You think I don't know what really happened?" He stretched in his seat, checking to make sure we wouldn't be overheard. "Please – Just tell me you know something."

I slid down against the wall, sitting on the concrete at the bottom of the ramp. "They took him yesterday and he was gone by this morning," I said. "That's all I know."

"Why?" he choked. "Why is he doing this to us? I've done everything he asked. Everything."

Mr. Weir broke down, and it took everything I had not to join him.

"I'm sorry," I whispered, not even looking at him as I said it. "I'm so sorry."

How much longer could all of this stay secret?

What would happen if Luke and I "disappeared" too? Would people start to realize that something was up? Or would the end of the world just tick by without anyone even noticing?

"Jordan!"

Luke's voice suddenly cut into my thoughts. I dragged myself to my feet and stepped away from the building.

Calvin was stomping down the road, pulling Luke with him. It still seemed wrong seeing him without a crutch.

I stood my ground. No point running, anyway.

Mr. Weir wheeled out from behind me, spinning around to meet Calvin as he arrived.

"What have you done with my son?"

Calvin looked down at Mr. Weir. The ghost of a smile crossed his face.

I took a swing, aiming to punch that smile straight down Calvin's throat.

Calvin's hand shot into the air, catching my fist before it hit home. He clamped down on it, crushing my fingers.

"Calm yourself, Jordan," he said, finally letting go. "You don't want to make me angry today."

He reached down to his belt and unclipped a set of keys.

"Come on. Let's go for a drive."

Chapter 20

Calvin took Luke and me the back way around the medical center. It was quieter out here. Less chance of us making a scene.

Mr. Weir tried to follow us until Calvin drew his gun and asked him to turn around.

We walked in silence, heading for the east end of town. Calvin in front, not even bothering to look back and check on us.

Luke's feet dragged along the bike path.

My body screamed at me to run – and my mind had to scream back just as loud how pointless that would be.

We reached the edge of town and turned up the

street bordering the bush.

There was a van parked about fifty meters away. Gleaming black, with a big red Shackleton Co-operative crest on the side. The van Reeve had used to bring us back from outside the wall, or one like it.

"Where are you taking us?" I asked.

No answer.

We stopped at the van, and Calvin unlocked the big double doors at the back. He shoved Luke roughly inside. I dodged out of the way before Calvin could touch me, and climbed in after him.

Calvin laughed and slammed the doors behind us.

We were crouched in an empty storage area. Pitch black, except for the tiny crack of light creeping in from under the doors. Nothing to sit on and no way to see outside.

"Peter's gone," I whispered.

"What?" hissed Luke's voice, right beside me. "What do you mean?"

"They've taken him from the medical center."

"When did this happen? I thought they were still –"

He was drowned out for a second as Calvin hit the ignition. The van began to move, and I braced my feet against the back of the door to keep from being pitched into it.

I felt Luke jolt forward beside me. There'd been three of us the last time we were in here, but it was still plenty cramped with two. We swerved around a corner, and I was thrown sideways into him.

"So, what – is that where we're going now?" Luke asked as we straightened out again. "To wherever they've got Peter?"

I shrugged. Then, realizing how useless that was in the dark, "I don't know. Why did Shackleton let you and me go if he was just going to capture us again? Why not just knock out all of our legs and be done with it?"

Luke grunted his agreement and the conversation died.

But I had a feeling we'd have an answer soon enough. The van shuddered and rocked. Calvin was moving fast. Wherever we were going, he was eager to get there.

After maybe ten minutes, we swerved again, and I could hear the *tink-tink-tink* of gravel spraying up against the sides of the van.

A couple more turns and the van began to slow. I rubbed my legs, trying to get rid of the pins and needles that were creeping into them.

Calvin brought us to a stop. His door opened and closed. There was a jingle of keys and then a sudden burst of light as he threw open the back to let us out.

I crawled outside.

We were at the airport.

It didn't look like anything had changed. The whole place was still completely abandoned. Just an empty stretch of tarmac and a little gray terminal building.

Luke looked up into the sky, as though expecting to see something coming in for a landing.

Calvin snorted. "Idiot boy."

He led us across to the terminal building. The window I'd smashed on our last trip out here had been repaired. Typical Phoenix. Everything pristine, even in a place nobody was supposed to see.

Calvin found the key and unbolted the entrance.

"In you go," he said.

"What are you doing to us?" I said.

Calvin reached for his gun again. "In."

"You can't shoot us," said Luke shakily, walking through the door. "Mr. Shackleton said –"

"The situation has changed quite a bit since then, don't you think?"

The inside of the building was just the way I remembered it. An empty shell. Everything that wasn't cemented down cleared out right after the last of us moved here.

Calvin circled a dusty marble counter, crossing to a door labeled *STAFF ONLY.*

He pushed it open, bringing us into what I guessed had been the employees' staff room. Small, windowless, and just as empty as the rest of the building.

No Peter.

"Sit," said Calvin, closing the door behind us.

We sat down against the wall. Calvin put his weapon back into its holster and stood over us, arms folded in front of him.

"A few of my security staff have developed an unfortunate curiosity about you," he said. "I decided it would be more prudent to have this discussion out here."

I had a feeling the discussion was going to be a short one. Calvin isn't what you'd call a master conversationalist.

"Mr. Shackleton," Calvin continued, "is very interested to know the whereabouts of your friend, Peter."

What?

A weird smile crossed his face. Like maybe he knew more than he was letting on.

Or maybe he was just thinking about hurting us.

"What are you talking about?" said Luke. "Why would we know –?"

"It'd be a terrible shame if the two of you decided to be uncooperative in this matter," said Calvin in a voice that sounded like he didn't think it would be terrible at all. "It would be all the excuse I needed to finish what should've been done two weeks ago."

Calvin's hand crept down towards his gun again, and a terrible thought crossed my mind. What if he'd been the one who'd taken Peter? What if he'd done it without Shackleton's knowledge?

We'd seen Calvin walking up to the medical center yesterday afternoon. If anyone had the resources to sneak Peter out undetected, it was him.

He'd made no secret about wanting us dead. Maybe this was his chance.

"So," said Calvin. "Where is he?"

"We don't know!" said Luke. "How would we?"

"Jordan? Any thoughts?"

I froze, itchy with sweat, forcing myself to keep looking straight at him.

"Nothing?" said Calvin. He pulled out his gun and aimed it at Luke's head. "How about now?"

"No!" said Luke, cowering. "No ... please ..."

"Put it down!" I said, shifting forward.

Calvin swung the gun across to me. "I really don't think that's –"

He broke off. In the silence, I heard a gentle buzzing. Calvin's phone.

He switched his gun to his left hand and reached down to fish it out of his pocket.

"Yes, sir, what is it? ... Yes, I'm out there already ... Thank you, sir ... Yes, I'll question them now ... Of course, sir. I'll let you know." Calvin returned the phone to his pocket, looking frustrated.

Shackleton's seen that we're out here, I realized.

"Why are you even bothering with all of this?" Luke asked. "Why can't Shackleton just find Peter with his computer?"

Calvin's smile looked like it was about to return.

"Yes," he said. "Why indeed?"

He switched the gun back into his right hand. Luke flinched at the movement.

Calvin crouched down, bringing himself level with us. "Last chance," he said, the barrel of his gun drifting lazily back and forth between Luke and me. "Where is he?"

I felt myself starting to shake, almost crying again. Not fear, though. It was bigger than fear. Bigger than me getting shot. After all my visions, everything that had happened …

It couldn't end like this. It couldn't.

This wasn't what I was here for.

Calvin began to straighten up, pointing his gun at Luke's shoe. "Maybe just the toes to begin with," he said. "Something to –"

No.

I threw myself at Calvin before he could stand all the way up again. He swore, staggering, gun slipping from his hand. He caught it again, but at least now his finger was off the trigger.

Both of us still off balance.

I found the ground first and threw up my knee, catching him between the legs. He cried out, and we both went down. I had one hand clawing at his face and the other frantically trying to pin his wrist to the floor. Calvin's head smacked into the carpet and my thumb slipped into his mouth. He bit down hard, and I screamed, hand shaking, thumbnail digging into the roof of his mouth, and then –

Calvin stopped struggling.

His hands dropped to his sides and he relaxed his jaw, letting my hand free. I tensed, waiting for him to spring up again. His fingers loosened around the gun and I snatched it up, throwing it away across the floor.

"Luke, quick!" I said. "Get his legs. Make sure –"

I jumped as Calvin made a noise under me. A shallow, gasping breath. I glanced down at his face.

He was crying.

Sobbing. Saltwater bucketing down from his eyes. Shoulders shaking with the effort.

"I'm sorry ..." he choked. "I'm sorry ..."

I backed off, pushing up slowly from the ground, poised to come down on him in a second if I had to.

What?

It was a trick, surely – but why? He'd almost had me.

Calvin pushed himself up on his hands, scrambling out from under me. He sat there for a moment, wiping his eyes, then slowly stumbled to his feet.

I leapt up too, hands outstretched, eyes flashing down to the gun on the floor.

But Calvin seemed to have forgotten about it. He opened his mouth, closed it again, took another heaving breath and turned to the door.

"Should we … do something?" Luke whispered behind me, as Calvin walked out.

We followed at a distance, reaching the door just in time to see Calvin step out onto the tarmac. He climbed into the security van, heaved the door shut, and peeled away down the dirt road towards town.

Chapter 21

"My place?" Luke suggested, squeezing through the mass of people outside the front office.

"Probably best," I said. "I don't think my parents have quite recovered from Mike's little visit."

I'd walked to school today, so I hung back from the end-of-day crush to the bike racks, waiting for Luke to find his way out again. We were planning to pick through everything we knew about Peter's disappearance and see if we could work out what Calvin might have done with him.

Neither of us had brought up the obvious – that there was every chance Peter was already buried somewhere out there in the bush.

No way were we going down that road.

It was two days since Calvin had left us stranded out at the airport. We'd waited in the terminal building for a few minutes after he'd left – shell-shocked apart from anything else – then headed outside and started the long walk home. I'd buried his gun on the way back. One less weapon in the hands of the Co-operative.

There'd been no sign of Calvin since.

But if we'd been expecting what had happened out there to help anything, it looked like we were out of luck. Peter was still missing, and life in Phoenix seemed to be continuing as normal.

The blood screening was back up and running this morning, and by the end of the day, the whole school had been moved through Montag's testing booths.

I was still losing sleep over Mum's and Dad's attempts to sort things out with Ketterley. At the moment, they were waiting. When Dad's visit had failed to get them any closer to booking a flight, they'd sent off a few angry emails – one to Ketterley, one to Mr. Shackleton, and one to the *Herald* – but it wouldn't be long before they discovered that was another dead end.

Then what?

Luke finally managed to haul his bike free, and we joined the crowd heading into the town center. I kept a lookout for Calvin, not really expecting anything.

"Do you want food?" Luke asked as we passed the mall. "Doubt my mum's bought groceries since –"

"Hang on a sec."

Mike and Cathryn were over on one of the benches circling the fountain in the middle of town. They were sitting with their backs to us, staring down at something in Mike's hands.

I took off my bag. "Here, hold this."

Between Peter's disappearance and trying to keep my family safe, these guys had slipped off my radar a bit. But I wasn't about to pass up a chance to figure out what they were up to.

I crept forward, edging around the fountain, the noise of the water disguising my steps.

I crouched down behind the bench in time to hear Cathryn say, "If you won't, I will."

"Cat, we don't even know where to look," said Mike. I saw a hand stretch down, stuffing whatever he'd been holding into his bag.

"Pete's our friend," said Cathryn. "We can't just –"

"Shh!" Mike whispered. "We'll send a message to the overseers, okay? Bring them an offering. See if they can tell us anything. But I wouldn't –"

"Mmph! Wha' you doin'?"

The shock almost knocked me over. Tank was right behind me, a doughnut sticking out of his mouth and a grease-stained paper bag in his fist.

He reached for me with his other hand.

"Get lost," I said, whacking the hand away and getting up.

Cathryn was on her feet too, breathing hard. Mike slowly zipped up his bag and stood up to join us, like he was trying to show me how relaxed he was.

"Have you found something out about Peter?" I demanded. "Do you know where he is?"

"No," said Mike.

"I swear, Mike, if there's anything you're not –"

"We'd tell you," said Mike. "No – Seriously. I know what you think of us, but we want Peter back as much as you do."

"More," Cathryn muttered.

Tank shot her a confused look. He opened the paper bag and pulled out another doughnut.

"We should go," she said.

Mike nodded. "Yeah. See you tomorrow, all right?"

I didn't try to stop them. Luke came up as they disappeared, handing over my bag. "What was that?"

"Nothing," I said. "At least – I don't know. They're trying to figure out how to find Peter."

"Good luck to them," said Luke. "They know even less than we do."

"We still don't know *what* they know," I said, glancing around to make sure Peter wasn't listening in on our –

Then I stopped, remembering.

Ugh.

We continued down the street to Luke's, cold reality hitting me all over again.

It was a few minutes before I said, "They're going to ask their overseers about him."

"Right," said Luke. "Whatever that means."

"Yeah."

I'd dreamed about the overseers again last night. Giant and faceless and gleaming. They'd cornered me in the cave, pinning me to the wall, pulling back glowing hoods, suddenly transforming into Calvin and Peter, both weeping hysterically, asking me why I didn't love them.

We filled up the rest of our walk with small talk. Not that we didn't have more important things to discuss, but there's only so much time you can spend talking in circles about the end of humanity without losing your mind.

But as soon as we walked through the front door, we were dragged straight back to business.

A buzzing sound from the kitchen.

The coffee machine.

Luke's forehead crinkled.

There'd been no bike on the veranda. And Luke's mum was not prone to getting home early from work.

The buzzing stopped.

"Mum?" Luke called out, moving up the hall.

A male voice. "No, Luke."

Luke stopped dead. He slid over to the hall stand and unhooked an umbrella. He gripped it in both hands, holding it out in front of him like a spear. Another time and place, it would have been funny.

Luke took one step into the family room. He hesitated, comprehension dawning in his eyes. Then his face screwed up in disgust.

"She gave you a *key?*"

I walked in after him. Dr. Montag was sitting on the couch, setting a latte down on the coffee table.

"Do you really think I need a key from your mother to get inside your house?" said Montag.

"Get out," said Luke.

"Lower your weapon, Luke," said Montag. "I'm only here to deliver a message. Hear me out and I'll leave the two of you alone."

He gestured at the couch opposite him.

Luke looked at me.

Two of us, one of him. No way for him to call for help apart from his phone, and we could get that out of his hands if we needed to.

I nodded.

Luke leaned the umbrella against the wall and we sat down on the couch.

Montag picked up his coffee again.

"As you may or may not have gathered from your visit to the Shackleton Building," he said, shifting into the tone he used whenever he was explaining something to Mum about the baby, "the residents of Phoenix did not arrive here by accident."

"Of course not," said Luke. "The Shackleton Co-operative brought them here."

Montag shook his head. "What I mean is it's no accident that this *particular* group of people was selected to be part of our work in Phoenix. Every single one of you is here because you meet a particular set of genetic criteria."

I remembered the database of everyone in Phoenix that we'd found in the Shackleton Building, and the words *genetic suitability confirmed* flashed into my mind.

"What kind of criteria?" I asked, fully expecting him to ignore the question.

"Resistance to the effects of our Tabitha weapon," said Montag. "Under the right circumstances."

He took a sip of his coffee and something in his expression changed, like whatever he was warning us about was more personal than he'd been letting on.

"However," he said, "as I began analyzing the results of the limited blood testing we were able to conduct on

Friday, an … unexpected anomaly cropped up."

"Something to do with me," Luke guessed.

Montag leaned forward in his seat. I raised my hands, half-expecting him to leap out and attack. But he was just putting his coffee back down on the table.

"Luke … you are not a genetic candidate. I don't know how you got here, how you slipped through our screening process. But you should never have been permitted to set foot in this town in the first place."

He gave this a chance to sink in.

"Why are you telling us this?" I asked.

But Luke saw straight through him. "Because if I'm not a genetic whatever, then neither is Mum."

One look at Montag's face told me he was right on the money.

"You need to tell Shackleton what you've done with Peter," he said.

"What does that have to do with anything?" I asked.

"We haven't –" Luke began. "If we'd found a way to stop you tracking Peter, why would we still be walking around with our own suppressors –?"

"Don't," said Montag. "Don't do this to yourself.

I'll keep this situation under wraps for as long as I can. I'll even try to find a way for you and your mother to survive in the new world. But you need to keep your heads down. Shackleton is taking a particular interest in anyone demonstrating extreme or unusual behavior. You can't afford to put yourselves in either of those categories."

Bit late for that, I thought darkly.

"Forget it," said Luke. "Even if we did know where Peter was —"

"Need I remind you, Luke, that the only reason you are not dead already is that I managed to convince Mr. Shackleton that we couldn't afford to kill you?"

Luke lowered his eyes.

"All that has changed now," said Montag. "You and your mother are not supposed to be here. And the instant Mr. Shackleton finds that out, both of you will die."

Chapter 22

I pedaled hard down the dirt path, wind rushing at my face, sweat beading on my forehead. I was out here alone, riding to clear my head. Or to shuffle all the junk in my head around a bit, at least. I'd started at the south end of town, taking the long, curving bike path that wrapped around Phoenix and emerged again near the top of my street.

Another day gone. Still no Calvin. And still no more fallout from Peter's disappearance. If Shackleton really didn't know where Peter was, why hadn't he come after us by now?

Luke seemed to be taking Montag's news pretty well. As well as you can take something like that.

He was worried about his mum, but he seemed to figure that the only way to protect her was to deal with Shackleton.

A misty rain was starting to drift down through the trees. I was almost home. I could see the edge of the explosion site coming up on my right, still taped off. I found myself slowing to look.

Don't even think about it, Peter's voice whispered in my head. *One death wish at a time.*

If only it were that simple.

It was hard to see much from this angle. The crater itself was hidden by the trees, and most of the fire-damaged area was –

I swerved, gagging violently. Convulsing. The bushland melted together. I tried to move across to the side of the path, to get off my bike before I blacked out, but my hands wouldn't respond. My front wheel hit a rock or something and the bike slid sideways, falling out from under me.

I was gone before I hit the ground.

The rain evaporated and the sky turned murky gray – almost sunrise or just past sunset, couldn't tell which.

I lay on the ground, clutching my stomach and coughing, until finally it subsided enough for me to pick myself up again. I was bleeding. A big graze all up my left arm.

When was I?

The bush looked exactly the same as it had a minute ago. The security tape was still stretching out between the trees. Most of it anyway. The section right in front of me had been snapped, and was now lying on the ground.

But if the tape was here, I couldn't have gone more than a week and a half back – and probably not more than a few weeks forward either.

So why was I here? What was I supposed to see?

I looked up and down the path. No movement except the wind. No sound except –

BLAM! BLAM! BLAM!

I dropped to the dirt again.

Gunshots in the bush. They were coming from inside the taped-off area. I ran to the edge of the road, almost falling again as the world shuddered around me, and stared through the trees.

For a moment, everything went quiet.

Then strained breathing and crashing feet and suddenly, I came running out from the bush with Luke right behind me.

Another Jordan. A future Jordan.

She recoiled, seeing the security tape lying across the ground in front of her. And then a look of understanding crossed her face. She spun around, her back to me, and scanned the bush to her left. Searching.

She was hurt. Blood soaked up through a gash in the gray fabric of her T-shirt. Not a bullet wound, though. Surely there wasn't enough blood for that.

Luke was in even worse shape. Nose bleeding, face bruised, swaying like he might pass out.

"Come on!" he hissed. "What are you doing?"

The other Jordan looked through the trees for a second longer, then said, "This way!"

"Jordan – no – what if –?"

But the other me was already veering off into the bush again.

I ducked under the security tape, trying to see where they were headed. Too late. By the time the trees had all blurred back into place, the other Jordan and Luke had slipped away.

And then it was time to go. The bush swirled together again, a hurricane of green and brown. I lurched forwards, straight across the broken section of tape, closing my eyes against the rising nausea.

More footsteps.

Another figure crashing through the bush.

BLAM! BLA–!

Gone.

I hit the ground again, chest heaving. Cold rain on my face. Sudden brightness on the other side of my eyelids. I coughed a couple more times and opened my eyes.

Cathryn was standing over me.

She was a mess. Eyes red, cheeks streaked with mascara, clothes soaking wet.

Too wet for this light rain.

She'd been to the cave again.

"Are you okay?" she asked. Her voice was choked with tears – but clearly I wasn't the reason for that.

"I'm fine," I said, sitting up. "What are you doing here?"

"I was on my way home. You were just standing

there, looking out into the bush," said Cathryn. "And then you collapsed into the security line."

I looked down at the freshly broken tape on either side of me. I'd snapped it when I fell. Which I guess explained why it had been broken in my vision.

I clambered back out of the bush. My bike was still lying there in the middle of the road. I reached for the handlebars and heard Cathryn sob behind me.

Honestly. This was the week of random breakdowns.

I sighed. "What's the matter? Where are Mike and Tank?"

"Back at the cave," she sniffed. "Don't worry."

"I'm not worried."

"No, I mean –" Cathryn blinked hard, sending more tears streaming down her cheeks. "I have something to tell you. Something they can't hear."

I heaved my bike upright again. "What?"

She stared out in the direction of their cave and took another shuddering breath.

"I know who kidnapped Peter."

"Who?" I demanded.

Cathryn burst into tears again.

"Us," she croaked. "We did it. It was us."

Chapter 23

"You?" I said. "But Mike was the one who –"

Of course he was.

That was why Mike had been so desperate to find me the morning after Peter had disappeared. He'd wanted to make sure I got his version of the story first. And I'd fallen for it without even thinking.

Cathryn stood in the middle of the road, staring at her shoes, hand over her face, crying uncontrollably.

"Cathryn! Stop!" I demanded, shaking her. "Where is he? What are you doing to him?"

"I don't know!" she sobbed. "We haven't got him anymore. We were only supposed to get him out of town!"

"What do you mean *supposed to?*"

A bike shot past, swerving to miss us. The guy looked over his shoulder as he rode away, frowning at the broken security tape.

"We have to move," I said, pulling Cathryn by the wrist. "I can't stay out here."

She stumbled along behind me, breathing still ragged. Her bike was lying on the other side of the path. She picked it up and started walking.

"The overseers," she said. "They – It was part of our calling. They needed Peter. They needed us to get him for them."

"For what?" I asked. "Who are they?"

"They're – the ones in charge," said Cathryn.

"The ones who set up the cave," I said, checking that the path behind us was still clear.

"The cave is – It's a sacred place. For when they want to meet with us in person," said Cathryn. She wiped her nose with the back of her hand, a shadow of her usual immaculate self. "We have to wear blindfolds, though. No one's ever allowed to see them."

"Why not?"

She sniffled again. "Those are the rules."

"So you don't even know who these people *are?*"

"Mike says he saw them once," said Cathryn. Then her eyes widened, like she'd just admitted something dangerous. "It was an accident! He only saw them for like half a second. Off in the distance, across the lake."

"Two people dressed in white," I said.

Cathryn stopped, head twitching around, searching the trees like a startled bird. Like she thought they could hear us. "Please, I told you, we're not supposed to –"

"They live somewhere close?" I said, looking around. "Somewhere out in the bush?"

"Maybe."

"Maybe?"

"I don't know!" said Cathryn, voice getting shaky again. "We're not – You don't ask them questions like that."

"So you just do what they tell you, huh?" I said, pushing on down the path. "You just blindly follow whatever –"

"It's not like that! We do it because we're meant to do it."

"According to who?" I said. "You don't even know who you're following! You're talking about two people Mike might have seen for half a second out in the bush! And they tell you to abduct Peter, and you just do it?"

"We had to! It was our –"

"Your destiny?" I snapped. "You were destined to take him?"

Cathryn broke eye contact, staring down at the ground again. "There's no way you could understand."

"Then why are you telling me all this? If I'm too dumb to get it –"

"Because it's *Peter!*"

"Yeah, you probably should have thought of that before you took him."

Cathryn dissolved into another round of sobs.

"I can't do this anymore. I can't. I don't care if Peter's dangerous! I just ... He needs to be safe."

"Why were you even doing it in the first place?" I pressed. "If Peter's the one they wanted, why didn't they just send a message to him?"

"They said he wasn't chosen," said Cathryn.

"They didn't say why. Not until last week, anyway."

Last Monday at the locker, I realized.

"The letter we caught you with – that was them telling you to kidnap Peter!"

"It was my fault," she said. "I told them about those two people on your computer –"

"That had nothing to do with us, you moron!"

"That's not what they said. They told us Peter was dangerous. They wanted us to lure him out. Convince him to come out here with us and then leave him for the overseers. But all of that got screwed after you found the cave. And screwed again after Peter got taken to the medical center." A fearful look came over Cathryn's face. "The overseers went nuts when we told them. They made us sneak in there that night and get him."

Just like at the mall.

Whoever these people were, they must have had some kind of access to the town security.

"I didn't want to go," said Cathryn. "I didn't. But Mike and Tank wouldn't listen. And I knew what the overseers could do to us if we failed. So we went. There were still people in there, but not many. Peter was out cold on one of the beds. We got him out, but –"

She broke off, and it was a few seconds before she was able to continue.

"He woke up. We were bringing him out to – to the place where we were meant to leave him. Tank was carrying him. And Pete woke up and started fighting. Tank dropped him and – Pete's legs didn't work, but he was punching and shouting. Mike picked up a branch from the ground. Tank held his arms down and – and Mike hit him. Not just once. Not like a movie. He had to – He had to hit him like three times before …"

Cathryn's eyes squeezed shut, face twisting up with the memory of it.

"It was bad," she said. "Mike got him knocked out again, but – there was so much blood. Tank picked him up and we kept going. Mike carried the branch with him. Just in case. We got to the place and – we just left him there. Just lying down there, bleeding."

We'd both stopped walking again.

I was shaking, my whole body wracked with revulsion and rage, not knowing whether to throttle her or fall to pieces next to her.

"Where?" I said. "Where did you leave him?"

Cathryn raised an unsteady hand, pointing back the way we'd come. "Out – out there. Out where that explosion happened. They told us to leave him in the crater."

Chapter 24

"You sure this is what we want to do?" said Luke again, as we rode past the Shackleton Building after school the next day. "I mean, after what happened to –?"

"Don't," I said. "That was different. We're not asking him to do anything he's not allowed to do."

"Yeah, but –"

"And you're the one who said we couldn't do it alone."

"Yeah." Luke smiled wearily. "But I thought I was talking you *out* of something, not further into it."

I raised an eyebrow. "C'mon. You know me better than that."

When we'd gotten to school that morning, the

first thing I'd wanted to do was grab Mike, drag him out to the crater and make him show us exactly what had happened to Peter. But then Luke had politely suggested that we might not want to die today.

We couldn't go rushing in like that, not with Shackleton looking over our shoulders. And letting Mike and Tank (and through them, the "overseers") know what we were doing was probably not such a smart idea.

Assuming Cathryn hadn't already confessed about our conversation yesterday.

But if Mike and Tank knew anything, they were keeping it quiet. They'd kept to themselves all day, deep in conversation. Or as deep as conversation can be when Tank is one half of it.

Cathryn hadn't shown up to school. I'd spent all of English worrying they'd done something to her. But then her mum had emailed in to say she was "sick."

Then there was another mystery: Cathryn's confession was pretty solid evidence that she and the others weren't getting their orders from Shackleton after all. So how on earth had Cathryn been able to keep it all secret from her mum? How had she been sneaking around all this time without getting caught?

I guess even evil dictators have blind spots when it comes to their own kids.

"Besides," I said, resting my legs and letting the bike coast down the street, "I told you what I saw in my vision. We were out there at the explosion site, looking for him."

"We were out there getting shot!" said Luke.

"Shot at," I said. "Not shot. We were running."

Unless that blood on my shoulder really was a bullet wound.

There was a weird silence. Luke and I both looked at each other. Waiting for the smart-arsed comment that Peter wasn't there to give.

Luke sighed.

"I didn't just see that vision by accident," I said. "There's something out there and whatever it is, we're supposed to –"

I cut myself short, realizing how much I sounded like Cathryn.

Supposed to?

I'd called her a moron for following orders without bothering to ask who they were coming

246

from. And here I was, putting my trust in – What? A vision of the future? How was that any different?

Because your visions aren't telling you to abduct people and leave them for dead in the bush, I told myself. *And because, so far, the real world backs your visions up.*

"Maybe it was a warning," said Luke. "If you really think you're seeing all of this stuff for a reason, then who says the reason isn't keeping you alive?"

"What do you think we're doing this for?" I said, pointing down the street as we turned the corner. "Trust me, staying alive is definitely part of my plan."

Luke sank down on his bike seat. "I just hope we can actually stick to the plan this time."

We rode to the house, let ourselves in through the gate, and left our bikes on the lawn.

The Co-operative had put in a ramp in front of the house, leading up to the veranda.

We took the stairs and I rang the doorbell.

"What if he's not here?" said Luke.

"His bike's here."

"Of course his bike's here," said Luke, and I felt a stab of guilt.

The handle turned and the door opened.

Peter's dad rolled into the doorway. He looked warily at us. "Did something happen? Have you –"

"Can we come in?" I asked. This wasn't the sort of discussion you wanted to have on a doorstep.

Mr. Weir ran a hand down over his new beard, which had grown even more out of control since the weekend. He spun his chair around and rolled back up the hall. Luke shut the door behind us and we followed Peter's dad into the family room.

I saw that one of those chairlift things had been installed on the stairs, to let Mr. Weir up to his bedroom. The Co-operative was doing everything it could to make it look like they were helping.

Luke and I sat down. Déjà vu. Every house in Phoenix was like a tiny little alternate universe, almost but not quite the same as every other. We were sitting in exactly the same positions we'd been in for our chat with Dr. Montag at Luke's place.

Mr. Weir pulled up next to the couch opposite us. He glanced sideways, like he was considering shifting himself across, then changed his mind.

"All right," he said. "What's going on?"

I put my head in my hands for a minute, trying

to figure out where to start.

"You're right," I said. "We know what the Co-operative is doing out here. We know what really happened to you – and to Peter. And we know why."

Mr. Weir cursed under his breath. "And you waited until now to tell me?"

"We didn't want to put you in danger," said Luke.

"I'm in a bloody wheelchair!" Peter's dad shouted. "My son's been abducted! How much more danger –?"

"Mr. Weir, the last person we asked for help is in a coffin," I said. "Can you blame us for wanting to be careful?"

Mr. Weir's fury wavered for a bit as the words hit home. "Tell me," he said. "Tell me what you know."

"We can't," said Luke.

"Yes, you bloody well can!" said Mr. Weir, rolling forward until he and Luke were knee to knee. "You can tell me right now."

"Mr. Weir, please, that's not what we came to –"

"THEY HAVE MY SON!"

"No. They don't," I said. "That's why we're here. The Shackleton Co-operative hasn't got Peter. They're looking for him too."

"But we think we might know where he is," said Luke. "Kind of."

Luke made a face. He'd been doing that all day, every time he thought over the fact that our whole plan was based on Cathryn's vague descriptions and a vision of him and me running from gunfire.

But thankfully, Mr. Weir wasn't interested in the source of our information.

"Where?" he asked. "Who's got him?"

"We're not sure," I said. "But if we can get into the bush at the north end of town without Shackleton realizing, we might have a shot at finding out."

Peter's dad gave his wheels a tug, backing off from us a bit. "I take it that's where I come in."

I cringed. Whatever I might have said to Luke, this still felt way too much like asking Officer Reeve to get us into the Shackleton Building.

"It would be a massive risk," I said quickly. "If Shackleton realizes what you're doing –"

"I'm in," he said. "Whatever it is, I'm in. What do you need?"

His face was alive in a way I hadn't seen since Shackleton took his legs.

"We need someone to distract Shackleton," said Luke. "Keep him away from the computer in his office that tells him where we are."

"No worries," he said immediately. "I can do that. I'll get up early. Get into work before he does. Should be even less drama with Calvin on leave."

"What?" I said. "On leave where?"

"At home," said Mr. Weir. "He went in to see Montag on Saturday. The doc told him to take a few days off." His eyes went dark. "Destroying lives is stressful stuff, I guess."

"There's one other thing," said Luke. "For some reason, when Peter went missing, the Co-operative stopped being able to track his suppressor."

"Isn't that good news?" said Mr. Weir.

"For now, maybe. But if we find him, and his suppressor starts working again – If Shackleton sees that we've got him –"

"Mate, stop," said Mr. Weir, sounding uncannily like Peter. "One problem at a time."

He rolled forward again, almost smiling at us. "Let me worry about Shackleton. You just concentrate on getting my bloody son back."

251

We decided that we'd make our start at 5 a.m. It would be early enough to get a jump on Shackleton, but not suspiciously early for a busy Co-operative employee like Mr. Weir to arrive at the office. And hopefully it would be light enough by then to see our hands in front of our faces.

I filled in the rest of my afternoon drawing pictures with Georgia.

The homework was still piling up on my desk. But if everything went bad tomorrow, I wanted to know I'd spent my last few hours doing something worth doing.

Dinner was late. Mum and Dad had gotten an email back from Shackleton's secretary (Katie Reeve, still unknowingly working for the man who'd murdered her husband), which was basically all the same lies and stall tactics rearranged into new sentences.

They were both outraged, and spent ages talking around in circles about what to do next. I did what I could to calm them both down, but I could tell this was all going to spill over sooner rather than later.

One more thing to worry about once we'd gotten Peter back.

After dinner, I went upstairs and got myself organized for tomorrow. I packed pretty much the same backpack I'd put together for our trip out to the wall: food, water, flashlight, rope, notepad, pen, my old pocket knife with the half-broken blade …

The kind of packing that made Luke look at me like I'd come unhinged.

I laid out some clothes for the morning, deliberately avoiding the gray shirt I'd been wearing in my vision. Learning from the visions was one thing, but I wasn't about to start letting them control me. I chose greens and browns and then, remembering it was a school day, stuffed my uniform into my bag to put on later.

Life and death covert rescue mission. Then math.

I went out to say goodnight to Mum and Dad. They'd finally given up on the flight-booking debacle for the night. Dad was sitting on the couch, going over some meeting notes. Mum was lying against him, hands on her stomach.

"Night," I said, leaning into the room.

Mum stood up to give me a hug, the same weary expression still etched across her face. "Night, sweetheart. See you tomorrow."

The baby kicked against me, and I almost started crying.

I was going to get them out of here.

I was going to find Peter and stop Tabitha and take my family home.

I bent down to hug Dad, then went upstairs to see Georgia. She was lying on her bed, making shadow puppets in the glow of her night light.

"C'mere," I said, sitting down on the bed. "Give me a hug."

Georgia wriggled across the bed and squeezed me around the middle. "Love you, Jordan."

"Yeah. Love you too."

I sat there in the almost-darkness, soaking in that tiny moment of goodness in this nightmare place.

"Hey, Georgia, I might have to leave before you get up in the morning, okay?"

"How come?"

"Just something I need to do," I said. "You'll make sure Mum and Dad are okay, won't you?"

"Yeah."

I squeezed her again. "Thanks. Goodnight, Georgia."

"Goodnight," she mumbled, face pressed into my side.

I started to let go, and she snapped her head up to look at me. Puzzled, like she'd just heard me say something weird.

Then she frowned and patted me on the back. "I hope he's out there," she said. "I hope you find him."

Chapter 25

More dreams. More faceless ghosts chasing me
through town and out into the bush. Faceless, but
still breathing, and close enough for me to hear them.
Everything in slow motion. I tried to speed up, but
the air around me was heavy as water. I could feel their
arms stretching out behind me. Fingers grasping.

A dull buzzing under my pillow dragged me clear
of them. My old, useless phone, set to vibrate so it
wouldn't wake up the whole house. I turned off the
alarm, jolting wide awake as I remembered what it
was for.

4:45 a.m.

I got up, dressed in the dark, threw on my backpack

and headed for the door, checking the stairs on my way out to make sure everyone else was still asleep.

As soon as I was through the front gate, I crossed over the road to the bush side. Away from the streetlights. It was still too early for any normal person to be up, but Calvin had security on patrol through the night.

Just to make us all feel nice and safe.

We'd decided to meet out at the cemetery and cut across to the crater from that side. The last thing we needed was to run into some early-morning cycling nut. I walked across to the corner and started up the little trail through the bush.

At first, I thought the moonlight was going to be enough to see by. But as I got further from the glow of the town, I realized I'd probably need to risk using the flashlight, at least for a bit. I pulled it out and switched it on.

And then I realized my first mistake of the morning.

When I was getting dressed, I'd completely forgotten about the clothes I put out for myself last night. I'd just pulled a T-shirt and jeans out of the closet. A gray T-shirt. The one from my vision.

I half-considered turning back and getting changed.

Don't be stupid, I told myself. *It's just a shirt.*

A minute or two later, I was standing in the cemetery. I swept the flashlight around. No Luke.

I was about to switch it off when the light fell across Reeve's tombstone. Gleaming white marble. A bunch of flowers and a little plastic truck had been laid down in front of it.

I froze up, playing Reeve's death over again in my head. Replaying the funeral. His family weeping and Shackleton barely managing to hide his smile.

There had to be a bigger picture here. There had to be more than I was seeing, otherwise Reeve's death was just a waste. And I refused to live in a universe where that was how it worked.

I jumped as a hand brushed my back.

Luke. Green shirt, dark brown cords. Just like in my vision.

"Hey," he said. "You ready?"

I moved the flashlight away from the tombstone. "Yeah. Let's go."

There was security tape at this end too. It stretched halfway around the clearing, then ran away into the bush towards the bike track. Luke pulled it up and we stepped underneath.

"Can you turn that off?" said Luke. "If they're still guarding the crater, we don't want –"

"Yeah." I took one last look around, making sure we were headed in the right direction, then switched off the flashlight. But all the darkness in the world couldn't hide us if Mr. Weir couldn't keep Shackleton away from the tracking computer. "I hope Peter's dad knows what he's doing."

"I hope we know what we're doing," said Luke.

The first few minutes were slow. Stumbling blind through the bush. But eventually my eyes began to adjust enough to see the trees before I crashed into them. We crept forward, quiet as possible.

It was freezing out here. Cold enough to see my breath if it wasn't so dark. How had I come out here without a sweater?

Focus, I ordered myself. *You're way too distracted. You can't afford it.*

The next tree I touched felt different. Smoother.

I moved on, rubbing my fingers together. Something dry and powdery had come off on my hand. Ash.

We'd reached the edge of the burnt-out area.

A couple more steps and we were in a clearing. It was lighter here, out from under the shadows of the trees. A dim, hazy glow, like the sun was starting to think about rising.

I could see the dark shape of the crater only meters away, surrounded by a ring of black ground and the charred remains of trees. Shoots of grass were already springing up to fill the empty space.

"Doesn't look like anyone's here," Luke whispered, in a voice that said he was sure they must be out there somewhere.

I crossed the gap, crouching a meter before the edge of the crater. The sparking lights shooting out of it after the explosion had gone dead now. Nothing left but shadows. I thought I could see some lighter shapes jutting out from the sides, but I couldn't make out any of the details.

"Need the flashlight," I said, flicking it on again.

Luke spun around, ready to run. But nothing came to get us.

We were alone. Security tape would be enough to keep most people away, and the Co-operative didn't need guards to tell them if *we* came out here.

Luke bent down next to me and I shone the flashlight out across the crater. The beam hit the far side. The hole was smaller than I'd expected.

There was concrete sticking out from the dirt a little way down the crater wall. Thick and crumbling. I traced over it with my flashlight. It ran horizontally along the crater, a whole line of it. No, a ring of it. Broken up in places, but definitely a ring. Like a ledge, all the way around. And more concrete down at the bottom, lying half-buried in big slabs.

"A building," Luke whispered, pointing at the concrete just below us. "I think maybe – What if all that concrete used to be the roof of something? Like, if it stretched all the way across ..."

"Underground, you mean?"

"Yeah. Like one of the Co-operative's tunnels or something. Those big bits further down – they look like they might've broken off –"

"The explosion must've come from down there," I said, sweeping the flashlight around again, visualizing it. "Smashed through the concrete. And then it caved in."

"Yeah," said Luke. "Didn't Calvin say something about the ground being unstable?"

I stretched forward, trying to get a better look down at the foot of the crater. It was pretty deep, but the walls looked like they were sloped enough to climb.

"I want to go down there," I said. "I can't really see the bottom."

"I dunno," said Luke. "What if we get stuck?"

"Should be fine. Plenty of handholds."

"What if I get stuck?"

I got to my feet. "All right. I've got an idea."

I started walking around the edge of the crater, reaching into my bag as I went. Luke followed. I didn't need to see his face to know exactly what kind of exasperated look he was shooting at me.

We stopped when my flashlight beam hit the burnt hulk of a fallen tree. The same one I'd hidden behind to eavesdrop on Calvin and Shackleton, back when this was all on fire.

I pulled out my coil of rope and shoved an end down under the tree.

Luke sighed. He sat down and started pulling off one of his shoes.

"Probably don't need to do that this time," I said, climbing over to pull the rope out the other side.

"Oh." He put the shoe back on.

I tied the rope in a loop, pulling it tight around the tree. Then I unraveled the rest and threw it down over the lip of the crater.

"There," I said. "All sorted."

I shoved the flashlight into the pocket of my jeans, gripped the rope with both hands, and leaned back over the edge. My feet slipped down through the loose dirt at the top, hitting the concrete ledge a meter or so down. I grinned up at Luke, then jumped out past the concrete and continued down the slope. "See? No worries."

The crater was no more than ten meters deep. Probably more like five. I let my feet slide down the wall, digging them into the dirt only a couple of times to dodge bits of debris. Closer to the bottom, the slope got gentler. I dropped the rope and ran the last few steps down to the foot of the crater.

I pointed the flashlight up at Luke. "You coming?"

"Yeah," he said. "Keep shining the – *argh!*"

Luke slipped over the edge. He landed awkwardly on the concrete, then fell off again, thudding into the dirt wall below, still clinging to the rope. He stared down at me, squinting in the flashlight's beam.

"Come on!" I said, hoping he couldn't hear the laughter in my voice. "You're like halfway there!"

He sighed again, pushed out with his legs, and made his way down the rest of the slope, almost cutting himself on a nasty bit of pipe.

His feet touched the ground and he threw down the rope. "Why can't we ever go on a deadly mission to, like, a pillow factory or something?"

I turned around, shining the flashlight across the ground in front of us. Giant slabs of concrete stuck up out of the dirt, some of them almost as high as my head. There was other stuff too. Splintered remains of the trees that had once been up on top of all this. Half-melted bits of metal that looked like they'd been part of some pretty heavy-duty machinery. Maybe that was what had exploded.

I stepped out into the wreckage.

"Careful," said Luke. "The ground might not be

safe to walk on. We don't know how deep –"

"What part of this did you think was going to be safe?" I asked, climbing on top of one of the slabs.

I turned in a slow circle, taking it all in. This place was like something out of a disaster movie. Rubble everywhere. Everything still and dead.

Whatever all this used to be, whatever more there was of it, there was no way we were uncovering it without an excavator.

I jumped back to the ground and kept searching.

My right foot got caught on something and I lurched forward on my other leg, almost falling. I righted myself, then pointed the flashlight down to see what had tripped me.

A pale gray tree branch. Old and dry. Not burned like the rest.

Stained with blood. The weapon Mike had used to bash Peter's head in.

I picked it up, avoiding the red end. It was like a baseball bat.

"Hey, can you bring the flashlight over here a sec?" Luke had moved out past me. He was right in the middle of the crater, kneeling over another one of the concrete slabs. This one was lying almost flat in the dirt. "There's something on here, but I –"

I dropped the branch and shone the flashlight down over his shoulder.

"– Oh."

More blood.

The rain had washed away the worst of it, but the stains were still there, soaked into the concrete.

This was where they'd left him.

"Jordan …" said Luke. "There's a lot of blood here."

"No," I said. "No, I think maybe it just looks like a lot because the rain came and spread it out. It's probably just –"

"Jordan." Luke pulled on my arm.

"No, listen, he's fine. This is nothing. It can't be as bad as it –"

"Jordan," said Luke more urgently. "Look."

He was staring up at the lip of the crater.

Two silhouettes were staring straight back.

"You're dead," Tank called out of the darkness. "You are so dead."

"You know what, Tank?" said Mike. "You might actually be right this time."

266

Chapter 26

Mike and Tank jumped down into the crater, sliding feet-first down the steep dirt slope.

I glanced back at our rope. No way we'd get up there before they reached us.

No choice but to confront them.

Tank hit the bottom of the crater. He rolled forward, landing on his hands and knees, almost impaling himself on a jagged shard of something poking up out of the ground. Mike was right behind him. He landed slightly more gracefully, but only because there was less of him to hit the ground.

"We should probably get out of here," said Luke nervously.

I stayed where I was. "Not yet."

Mike and Tank strode over. Tank was dressed in his black shoplifting clothes, but Mike was wearing an old T-shirt and flannel pajama pants. His hair was a mess and he looked like he'd finished waking up on the way over.

Which means they weren't planning on being out here, I realized.

One of them must have seen us sneaking out. Tank, I assumed, since he was the one who was dressed. He must've run to get Mike and dragged him straight out to find us.

Mike stopped a few meters short of Luke and me. He reached down and grabbed the branch with the blood on it.

"You going to try that on us too?" I asked. "Or do you only beat up people who can't walk?"

"Who told you?" Mike demanded.

He turned to Tank, who backed away, frantically shaking his head. "Mate, you know I would never –"

Mike wheeled back around to face me, eyes bulging. "Cathryn?"

"Yeah," I said. "Apparently watching Peter's face

268

get smashed in was a bit much for her. Who would've thought?"

"Oh, mate," said Tank, suddenly panicked, "she's gonna die. They're gonna kill her."

"You think she didn't know that?" yelled Mike. "You think she doesn't know what happens if we fail them? What's the first command they gave us?"

"It all has to stay a secret," said Tank.

"Which means even if we don't like what they tell us to do," said Mike, "we keep our freaking mouths shut!"

"Yeah, but …" Tank frowned, like he was trying to say something more complicated than he had the words for. "They didn't tell us to hurt Pete. We just did it."

"We had to!" said Mike. "What choice did we have?"

Tank didn't seem to have an answer to that one. "So what now?" he asked.

Mike looked uncertainly at the branch in his hand. "Now we have to finish it."

He leapt forward, swinging the branch at my head. My flashlight thudded into the dirt as I threw my arms up to block it. The branch slammed into the side of my left hand, sending pain rocketing up my arm. My right hand closed over the end of it, over the patches of dried blood, and I pushed it back, straining to keep it away from my face.

I glared at him. "What's the plan here, Mike? You going to kill me?"

"No," he said. "We're going to leave you for the overseers. Let them decide what do with you."

A thump and a shout from a few meters away. Tank had Luke pinned against a chunk of concrete.

Ignoring the screaming pain in my fingers, I grabbed on to Mike's branch with my left hand and tried to twist it away from him.

Luke shouted again. I looked back in time to see the dark shape of Tank's fist drawing back from a punch to Luke's head.

I twisted the branch again, angling my arm up to elbow Mike in the face. He snarled, holding on tight.

Tank's fist came down and there was a dull thud as Luke's head got knocked back against the concrete.

"Get off him!" I shouted, like that was ever going to do anything.

I elbowed Mike again, then heaved back on the

branch, throwing him off balance. I grabbed a fistful of his hair, trying to pull him to the ground. He shouted, toppling forward onto one leg.

Luke was flailing and kicking, but Tank was way too big for him. A couple more blows and he'd be gone.

I drove a knee up into the side of Mike's leg, hard as I could, and he finally dropped. He knocked me back into the dirt, landing right on top of me. I let go of the branch. If he'd been a few seconds quicker, Mike could've smacked it down across my head and it would all have been over. But he hesitated just long enough for me to roll him off and pin him to the ground. I dug a knee down into Mike's back and tore the branch out of his hands.

Another cry of pain. But this time it was from Tank. Luke must have gotten him. I glanced over as Tank reeled away, a hand to his eye, then swung back his arm for another punch.

"Tank, WAIT!" I yelled, grabbing one of Mike's flailing hands and yanking it up towards me.

Tank turned to look. His fist hung in the air.

"Hit him one more time and Mike's arm comes out of its socket!"

I gave Mike's arm a tug, trying to convince them both that I meant business.

Mike yelped. "Don't just stand there, you idiot!"

Tank rushed over.

Which was lucky, because I didn't have the first clue about how to dislocate a shoulder.

Luke staggered up from the concrete, holding his head. Blood was bubbling down from his nose.

"Run!" I yelled.

"No," said Luke, spitting out what was probably more blood. "I'm not –"

"Trust me!"

Luke shot me a pleading look, then ran off through the rubble, towards our rope.

"Back off!" I warned, catching a glimpse of Tank's hands coming down.

Tank raised his hands up into the air, completely at a loss. "Mike?"

"GET HER OFF ME, YOU FREAKING MORON!"

"Back away, Tank!" I said. "Right back to the edge of the crater, or I swear I'll –"

Tank snatched Mike's branch up from the ground.

"Don't," I said, bending Mike's arm further back. "Don't even –"

"DO IT!"

The branch came down hard across my back. I screamed as a jagged bit of wood drove its way into my shoulder, tearing a hole in my shirt.

Tank drew back the branch and I collapsed down on top of Mike.

There was a sickening crack.

Mike howled in pain.

I'd come down right on top of his arm, snapping it flat across his back, up over the opposite shoulder.

Accidentally following through on my threat.

Mike screamed again as Tank grabbed me roughly by the back of the shirt, dragging me off. I caught a fleeting glimpse of the mangled arm before he shoved me facedown into the dirt.

"Mike!" he said. "Are you okay?"

"DOES IT LOOK LIKE I'M OKAY?"

I jumped up and bolted, grunting at the pain in my shoulder, but knowing it was nothing compared to Mike's. I almost ran straight into Luke, who'd been standing at a distance, watching.

"What are you waiting for?" I hissed. "Move!"

We ran for the rope.

"You broke his *arm?*"

"It was an accident!" I said, feeling the blood soaking through the back of my shirt.

"NO!" yelled Mike behind us. "YOU THINK YOU CAN FIX A BROKEN ARM? GO GET THEM!"

"Crap," said Luke, reaching the rope first.

Luke pulled the rope tight and started walking up the dirt slope, digging his feet in with every step to keep from slipping. As soon as he was up above my head, I grabbed the rope behind him. My shoulder burned as I pulled with my right arm, and I almost fell back down again. Tank's lumbering form burst out behind me. I shoved the pain aside and kept climbing.

"Hurry!" I said as Tank made a grab for my foot. I kicked at his fingers, pulling myself out of reach just in time.

Luke was almost halfway up, but the slope got steeper at the top. He was slowing down.

I felt the rope move below me. Tank had just picked it up.

But he wasn't climbing.

He started jerking the rope, yanking it back and forth, trying to knock us down. Every movement sent another blast of pain up my arm.

A grunt from above me. Luke lost his footing, kicking dirt down on top of me. He slid, feet scrabbling against the slope, until one of them finally caught on the bit of pipe that had almost sliced him open earlier. He straightened out and kept climbing.

I heard unsteady footsteps on the ground below, and ragged, heavy breathing. It sounded like Mike had finally gathered the strength to get up and join us.

"What – are – you – *doing?*"

"Shaking 'em off," said Tank.

"No – get up there!" Mike commanded, unable to get through a sentence without wincing. "Grab Jordan! Luke won't leave – without her."

The rope pulled tight below me. I looked down. Tank was on his way. He wasn't exactly agile, but he was the only one of us who hadn't been injured this morning, and he was getting up the rope surprisingly quickly.

Luke had made it as far as the concrete ledge. He pulled himself up, stretching a foot over to the dirt on the other side.

And then the whole rope shifted backwards.

Luke dropped back, scraping his leg on the concrete.

The fallen tree. Strong enough for one or two of us. Not three. Not when one of them was Tank.

It was moving.

"Tank, get off!" I shouted down at him. "There's a tree up there! You're going to pull it down on top of us!"

The rope shifted again.

The sudden drop made Tank slip, but he righted himself and kept climbing.

I stared at the concrete above me. Luke was still only halfway over. I climbed up as close as I could get behind him and latched on to the narrow ledge with my left hand. I found a foothold on a piece of debris and abandoned the rope, swinging my other hand up to the concrete.

My legs worked furiously against the dirt, pushing my body up far enough for me to get a good grip with my hands. I straightened my arms, groaning at the fire in my shoulder, and hauled myself up onto the concrete.

Luke was teetering on the ledge, still holding the

rope for balance. I stood up next to him, just in time to see the fallen tree lurch closer to the edge again.

"Crap!" said Tank, right below us, letting go with one hand.

Luke stumbled, jerked back by the rope, his foot slipping off the edge of the concrete. I caught him by the shirt, almost letting go again as my shoulder threatened to tear itself apart.

"NOW!" said Mike. "GRAB ONE OF THEM!"

Tank's fingers were straining for the leg of Luke's pants. One tiny yank and we'd come straight down on top of him.

I clawed at the wall with my other hand, but there was nothing to hold on to. I swayed backwards, coming away with a handful of earth, and the two of us reeled over the edge.

My hand flashed out. Closed on the rope again.

I pulled.

The tree scraped another half-meter closer, then lodged itself in the dirt.

I twisted the rope over my good shoulder and heaved. The tree wobbled but stayed where it was. Slowly, I dragged us back to vertical. Luke got his foot back up on the ledge, and the two of us clambered up over the lip of the crater.

Half a dozen flashlight beams swarmed down on us.

I got to my feet, squinting, disoriented.

And in those ten seconds of lost concentration, Tank hoisted himself up between Luke and me, grabbing hold of both of us.

"Hey, Mike!" he said. "I got – Huh?"

"Hold those two right there, young man," called a cold voice from across the crater, "and I will consider overlooking your breach of the curfew."

Officer Calvin was back on duty.

Chapter 27

THURSDAY, JUNE 25
49 DAYS

Calvin's men split up. Two of them followed him around one side of the crater, and the other three started circling in the opposite direction. Whatever had happened to him out at the airport, it had well and truly worn off by now.

"Tank!" hissed Mike from down in the crater. "What's going on, man?"

"Tank, please," said Luke, "you have to let us go."

But Tank was too focused on the approaching guards to answer either of them.

I tried to pull free, but every time I moved, it was like someone was jabbing a fork into my shoulder. My shirt was wet with blood, and the fabric rubbed against the wound, making the pain even worse.

We get away, I thought desperately. *We get away.*
I saw it in the vision.

But who said things had to play out the way I'd
seen them? Maybe it was already too late for that.
Maybe we weren't supposed to let ourselves get caught
in the first place.

The guards were closing in now. As Calvin got
nearer, I noticed a new addition to his security chief's
uniform. Tight-fitting gloves, the same bright red as
the Phoenix logo on his chest.

He saw me looking at them.

"Yes," he said, holding up a hand. "I don't know
what you did to me out there, but rest assured, it is
not going to happen again."

Calvin's meltdown in the airport. It had happened
when he bit my finger. He thought it was me.

How do you know it wasn't?

But I abandoned the thought as Calvin drew his
gun and pointed it at Tank.

Tank's giant fingers clenched around my arm.
"What? No – I'm helping! I'm helping!"

"Sir?" said one of the guards.

"Tell me about Tabitha," Calvin demanded. "Tell me everything you know about Tabitha and I'll spare your life."

"Who is she? I don't know anything!"

"Tell me!"

"I don't know!" Tank whimpered. "Please! Please! I don't know! I swear I don't know!"

He cowered and shook, holding on to Luke and me like we were keeping him alive. Calvin let him grovel for another few seconds. Then he lowered the gun. "Good."

Tank's knees gave out from under him. He let go of us and collapsed to the ground, gasping and weeping.

By now, the five other security guards had formed a tight circle around us and Calvin. Barnett, Miller, and three others I only half-recognized.

"Get up," said Calvin, giving Tank a kick. "Get up and go home. And if you tell anyone what you've seen here tonight —"

"I won't!" said Tank, rising shakily to his feet. "I promise. I promise." He pushed his way through the circle and lumbered off into the darkness.

"Sir," said one of the guards, perched over the crater with his flashlight. "There's another kid down here."

"Help!" called Mike. "Help me!"

Calvin stepped closer to the edge.

Close enough for me to push him in.

Luke caught my eye, guessing what I was thinking. He shook his head.

I shrugged at him. *Do you have a better idea?*

Luke glanced at Officer Barnett.

Even if we did knock Calvin into the crater, there was no way we were getting past five other guards. All we'd be doing was giving him another reason to hurt us when he got back out again.

Calvin shone his flashlight down into the crater. "What happened to you?"

"She broke my arm!" Mike groaned.

I shouted back down at him. "It was self-defense!"

"Can you get out?" asked Calvin.

"No," said Mike. "I don't think so. Please, chief – I need –"

"Turn around and walk to the other side of the crater," said Calvin.

"But –"

"Walk to the other side. Sit facing the wall. And stay there until I tell you otherwise."

"Chief, it really hurts."

"MOVE!"

Mike fell silent. I heard him shuffling away to the other side of the crater.

He's getting rid of the witnesses, I realized. *Making sure no one sees what happens next.*

"All right," said Calvin, rejoining us. "Back to business."

"You want us to take them back for questioning, sir?" asked one of the guards.

Calvin ignored him.

"Let's see," he said, counting off our supposed offenses on his gloved fingers. "Kidnapping a patient from Phoenix Medical. Breaking curfew. Entering a restricted area. Assault on a fellow student. It's a pretty condemning list of charges, isn't it?"

"Like you need one," I said.

"No," Calvin smiled. "Not out here."

He raised his gun.

"Chief!"

"Quiet, Miller!" Calvin barked.

He aimed the weapon at my stomach. Not interested in ending it quickly.

He wanted me to feel it.

"No Montag to save you this time."

How fast could I jump down into the crater?

Not fast enough. And even if I somehow got over the edge in time, Luke would be dead before I landed.

"Sir," said Miller, "Mr. Shackleton's orders were to –"

"Shackleton doesn't know we're out here," said Calvin. "This is just between us."

"But they're just *kids*," said Miller.

"They are a danger to *everything* we're doing here!" Calvin shouted.

Keeping the gun pointed firmly in my direction, he turned to survey his men.

"If any of you are not comfortable with this," he said sharply, "now would be a good time to walk away."

A long silence.

One of the guards I didn't recognize backed out of the circle. He turned, shaking his head, and started back around the crater.

BLAM!

He fell to the ground.

I didn't even have time to flinch before Calvin's gun was trained on my gut again.

Luke jerked next to me, gagging. He swallowed hard, fighting to get it under control.

"Anyone else?" Calvin asked.

The guards stared at him in shock. Even Barnett was looking like this was all a bit much for him.

I stepped back, heels almost hanging over the edge.

"All right then," he said. "Let's get to it."

No! This isn't supposed to –

BLAM!

Luke cried out. I opened my eyes.

Miller had grabbed Calvin from behind, dragging him back by the face. It looked like he was trying to disarm Calvin without hurting him, but Calvin was fighting back way too hard to let that happen.

"SHOOT HIM!" Calvin screamed. "SOMEBODY!"

Luke stared at me, still trying to work out which one of us had taken the bullet.

"Run!" I shouted, pulling him with both hands. "Luke – RUN!"

Chapter 28

We ran. Straight through the gap Officer Miller had left in the line when he'd launched himself at Calvin. One of the other officers tried to step in front of me, but I dodged past him and charged into the bush, glancing back one last time to see Barnett wrapping his arms around Miller, trying to pull him off.

Past the edge of the clearing. We were heading north, away from town. Not that it mattered much where we running right now, as long as it was putting distance between us and Calvin.

Luke was struggling to keep up. Not as fast as me at the best of times, and probably concussed from Tank's beating. But he kept moving.

BLAM! BLAM!

More gunshots from back at the crater. I heard a roar of pain, but couldn't tell who it had come from.

Crashing movement behind us. Flashlight beams. The other two guards were giving chase. They might not have been willing to shoot us, but they'd seen enough to guess what Calvin would do to them if they let us get away.

The bush was thick up ahead, the ground crowded with rocks and bushes and more spiny knee-high grass. Shadows on shadows. A million things to trip on.

I took one look at Luke, who was half-running, half-limping. No way we could outrun the guards through all that. I darted away to the right.

"Stop!" ordered one of the guards. "Phoenix Security!"

Yeah, that'll work.

I surged forward, pain rattling through my shoulder with every step. The terrain in this direction wasn't much better. The grass was gone, but the trees grew close together, and there were rocks littering the ground, waiting to trip us up.

I caught a flash of light over my shoulder. The guards were gaining.

In front of us, a giant old tree had come down across a couple of boulders. There was a gap underneath. Impossible to tell how big it was in the gray light. Would that be faster than going around?

I took a chance, diving down between the branches, gasping with pain as my right hand hit the ground. I pulled myself through, fingers clawing in the dirt. I jumped as a hand brushed my leg. It was Luke, coming after me. I yanked him to his feet and we kept running.

The two security officers reached the tree. Circuited around it. It wasn't much, but it bought us a few more meters.

I scanned the bush. No plan. There was no going back to town now. Nothing to do but keep running and hope –

A blur of black to our right, darker than the shadows. Officer Calvin had broken free and was cutting across to meet us.

For a second, I lost focus. My foot hit a rock and I flew forward. I waved my arms, desperately trying to get my balance back.

I grabbed at a branch in front of me, caught

myself, and kept running. Luke was a few steps behind me now. He kept looking back, fixated on Calvin. It was slowing him down.

"Ignore him," I said.

"*Ignore him?*" he panted. "Are you –?"

BLAM! BLAM! BLAM!

I could hear the other guards behind us. Calvin had stopped moving to line up his shot, but he was after us again. I thought I'd been running as fast as my body would let me, but it's amazing what you can pull out when someone starts firing a gun at you. I ripped through the trees, Luke right behind me now, finally managing to get some more distance on the guards.

But then we ran out of trees.

We'd hit the bike path. I recoiled, jarred by the sudden lack of cover. I looked down into the dirt and saw the broken line of red security tape lying on the ground in front of me.

And suddenly, a million things rushed into my brain at once.

The crater. The explosion. The ground caving in. Slabs of old, crumbling concrete. And then the building from my vision. The one with the spiral on it.

Concrete. Out here in the bush. Before there was any bush. Closer to town than the crater, but not by much.

It all flashed past in about two seconds.

I spun around, scanning the trees to my left.

What if they were connected? What if that was why I'd seen it?

What if that building was still there?

"Come on!" Luke hissed. "What are you doing?"

I took one more second, trying to gauge where the building should be, then sprinted back into the trees. "This way!"

"Jordan – no – what if –?"

But he was already following. We ran deeper into the bush, bashing through the long grass or reeds or whatever that had suddenly cropped up again.

BLAM! BLAM!

I looked back, but couldn't spot Calvin.

Could he actually see us or was he just taking potshots in the dark?

I strained forward, trying to block out the all-too-rational voice in my head telling me there was no way that building was out here, that it was too close to the town, that it would've been discovered ages ago. Asking me why I was pinning all our hopes on a crumbling old building anyway.

A second later, I was hurtling to the ground. I'd kicked a root or something buried in the grass. We'd come to the top of another slope, and I tumbled downwards, making enough noise to let the whole world know where I was. I rolled to a stop, grass towering above my head.

"Over here!" shouted one of the guards, close behind.

Luke appeared, thrusting out a hand to pull me up. I took it with both hands and dragged him down instead.

"Jordan –"

"Shh!"

No time. I'd cost us too much ground. Our best shot was to stay as still as possible and hope they missed us in the dark.

Crunching movement from two directions as Calvin and his men closed in. Flashlight beams flickered above our heads. The sounds grew louder.

Calvin's head and shoulders appeared above the grass. I held my breath, sure we were dead.

But he hadn't spotted us. Not yet, at least.

"Sir?"

"Go," Calvin ordered. "Find them."

More crunching as the guards waded away through the grass. Calvin stayed right where he was. He waited until they were gone, then pulled his phone out of his pocket, snapping the last thread of hope I had left.

He was calling Shackleton.

Getting him to pinpoint our position.

Asking him to activate our suppressors.

Then all we'd have left would be to see how long we could hold in the screams.

Silence as Calvin waited for Shackleton to answer. Every second felt like ten. I could feel Luke shivering next to me.

The footsteps of the other officers had faded away. Just him and us now. But Calvin wasn't letting his guard down. Not this time. He held the phone in his left hand, gun still at the ready in his right.

More silence, impossibly long.

Calvin gave a sudden growl of frustration. He pulled the mobile from his ear, screaming down at it. "Answer your bloody phone!"

My mind struggled to catch up. I was so used to our plans going wrong that, for a minute, I couldn't see what was right in front of me.

Mr. Weir. He must've had Shackleton distracted somewhere public, where he couldn't answer his phone.

Calvin tried the phone again. He stood with his back to us, shining his flashlight around in the grass, grumbling.

Another five seconds. Or fifty.

Calvin ripped the phone away again, jamming it back into his pocket.

He stomped off through the grass to find his men.

I stretched up, sticking my head just above the top of the grass. I counted four flashlights. It looked like Barnett had caught up with the search, which was probably bad news for Officer Miller.

They were all around us. But spread out. None of them closer than twenty meters.

I waved a hand at Luke, gesturing for him to get up.

"Now what?" he whispered.

I pointed down the slope, in the direction where the building from my vision was supposed to be. A path that would take us down between two of the flashlight beams.

Luke grimaced, but didn't argue.

We continued downwards, going for stealth instead of speed this time, keeping a close watch on the flashlights. At the bottom of the hill, the grass gave way to a patch of denser trees and scattered, spindly bushes. We picked up the pace, taking cover behind the bigger trunks.

I stared through shadows. Still no mysterious building.

Luke froze. We'd come level with the two guards. One on each side of us.

The guard on the right was sweeping his flashlight across in our direction. There were plenty of trees between us and him, but a lucky glimpse at the right angle would still be all it took.

I crouched at the root of a tree.

The light swept past us. Stopped. Swept past again.

The guard turned and continued his search in the other direction.

We kept going.

I felt the panic starting to well up in my chest. We had to be almost back to town by now.

What if I was wrong? What if there was nothing out here? And even if there was, we couldn't keep running forever. It was only a matter of time before Calvin got in touch with Shackleton.

I glanced back at the flashlight beams. They'd formed a search line. All four of them were sweeping towards us. Trying to flush us out. I sped up, nearly stacking it on a hunk of pale rock looming up in front of me.

Why had I started trusting those visions in the first place? Because they'd shown us where to find Reeve?

Look where he'd ended up.

"Ow!" Luke muttered. He was right behind me, rubbing his shin where it had collided with the rock I'd just stepped over.

But it wasn't a rock.

It was concrete.

A whole ragged line of it, running through the bush. I bent down, following it. After maybe fifteen meters, the concrete suddenly got taller, stretching up to almost shoulder height. It turned a corner, bending at a right angle and then sinking down into the ground.

"Walls," I whispered, rounding the corner. "These used to be walls! This was a building!"

"Yeah, great." Luke eyed the flashlights shining closer.

He stopped as a weirdly familiar noise broke out from the other side of the concrete.

A hiss of compressed air.

I checked to make sure the guards hadn't been close enough to hear, then jumped over the remnant of the wall.

Inside, the ruin was completely overgrown. There were trees almost as tall as the ones outside, and the ground was covered in grass and dirt and leaves. This place had been abandoned for a long time.

The hissing stopped, replaced by a rattling, clunking sound.

"Jordan," said Luke, pointing. "There!"

A few steps away, in the shadow of another half-destroyed wall, a perfectly square section of grass and dirt had just finished lowering itself into the ground, and was now sliding away into the side of a long, dark tunnel.

Chapter 29

The square of earth finished shifting aside. Like the trapdoors under the town, but older and clunkier.

I squatted down to peer into the tunnel, blocking out the sounds of Calvin and his men rustling through the bush around us. I could just make out the first couple of steps leading down into the darkness. Damp, moldy concrete instead of glimmering steel.

"Jordan," Luke whispered. "Is this –? Do you know what this is?"

I sat down, throwing my feet over the edge, hope swelling again. "Nope. Come on."

"What if it's one of theirs?" asked Luke, but he

was already crouching down to follow me.

I dropped through the gap and started down the steps. They were spongy with the damp, but they seemed stable enough – until one of the guards yelled out behind me and I almost slipped.

"Sir!"

Luke raced down after me. The missing section of dirt had already begun sliding back out of the wall, and he had to duck to get out of its way. Just as it was sealing shut, I saw a beam of light swing through the sky above us.

And then it was gone.

We stood on the steps, listening.

"Over here!" called Barnett, voice muffled by the dirt.

"Where?" snapped Calvin. He had to be standing right on top of the entrance.

"I – I thought I saw Hunter sitting down here somewhere."

"Sitting," said Calvin. "Just waiting for us to come and pick him up, was he?"

"Sorry, sir. I'm just telling you what I –"

"FIND THEM!"

I kept going, heart beating again. Calvin hadn't guessed where we'd gone. Which meant whatever we were walking into, the Shackleton Co-operative hadn't built it.

And then something else occurred to me.

What if Peter's down here?

Already I could tell that this staircase went deeper than the one in Pryor's office.

What if that was why the Co-operative hadn't been able to find him? What if he was too far underground, out of range of Shackleton's tracking computer?

What if we weren't completely screwed after all?

The stairs ran down in a tight spiral. I reached out to the right, but there was no handrail to keep us from falling over the edge. I held my left hand to the grimy wall to keep on track, trying to ignore the sudden mental image of a floating white giant seizing my ankle and dragging me away into the darkness.

I started counting steps to distract myself. After about fifty, I noticed a dim light glowing from somewhere below us. Not enough to see by, but it probably meant we were getting close to the bottom.

Ten more steps and I staggered forward, expecting another stair but hitting the floor instead.

"Careful," I said, as Luke stepped down behind me. "We're here."

"Right. Wherever that is."

There was a door across the room. It was open a crack, letting in a little light. I tiptoed across and peered through the gap.

A hallway. Peeling paint. Dirty floor. Dim, flickering light coming down from the ceiling. All quiet, except for a faucet dripping somewhere out of sight.

Empty.

We went through.

There was a row of doors to our left. I pushed open the first one.

The room on the other side was long and narrow. There were about a dozen beds inside. Steel frames, beginning to chip and rust. At some point, I assumed, the beds had been lined up in rows along the walls, but now they'd all been shoved to the back of the room, piled up on top of each other.

All except one. The remaining bed stood in the middle of the cleared space, surrounded by a few rusting lockers and some scattered clothes. The bedsheets were clean and white – out of place in the middle of all this decay.

Someone still lived here.

I shut the door again, careful not to bang it, and moved along the hall to the next room.

It was almost the exact same setup. A pile of beds at the back, and a makeshift living space for one person at the front.

"What happened to the rest of them?" Luke said.

My first thought was Shackleton.

But whatever this place was, it was way older than anything the Co-operative had built. So maybe the real question was what was anyone still doing here?

I put my ear up to the next door. The dripping was coming from through here. I reached for the handle.

A bathroom. Three toilets and a couple of shower stalls. Dirty, but not as gross as they could be. Someone was at least trying to keep on top of the mold.

Water was splashing down into one of the sinks in the corner. I went over and wrenched at the faucet. There was a loud squeak of metal and then the room went silent.

"Why aren't they coming for us?" Luke whispered as we backed out into the hall again. "Whoever's down here –"

"Maybe they're not home," I said.

There was another door opposite us, slightly ajar.

"Then who let us down here in the first place?" Luke asked.

I pushed the door the rest of the way open.

"Whoever it was," I said, looking inside, "I think I've figured out how they saw us coming."

The room was small and cramped. Shelves lined the walls in front of me, stacked with document folders and old video tapes, all neatly ordered and labeled. An ancient TV and VCR sat on a desk in the corner, beside another door.

In the middle of the room was a big, round table, covered with a circle of laptops that looked way too new for this place. They were Phoenix standard issue, all switched on, each one showing a different stream of video.

Video of the town.

Somehow, these people had hijacked Calvin's security feeds.

Two chairs were parked in front of the screens. I rolled one of them out and sat down.

I looked down on the food court, empty except for a cleaner mopping the floor. The welcome center in the Shackleton Building, just starting to come to life for the day. The security center, still quiet. Obviously word hadn't gotten back to them about this morning yet.

No footage from the medical center. In all of my trips, I'd never seen a single security camera in that place. I was sure there was a reason for it, but in a town as security-obsessed as Phoenix, it just didn't seem to –

"Uh … Jordan …?"

I spun around on the chair.

Luke was staring at the wall behind me.

Giant bulletin boards ran from one end to the other. They were crammed with bits of paper, all precisely arranged and linked together with different colored bits of string. There was empty space left at the right-hand end, like this had all been built up over time and was still being added to.

Photos, newspaper clippings, printouts from the

security screens, emails, Post-it notes, maps covered in pins. All with one thing in common.

Us.

Luke, Peter and me. Everything the Co-operative had ever printed about us since we got here – and plenty they hadn't – all collected and sorted and staring down at us.

I stood up, and started walking along the wall. The timeline stretched all the way back to the day I'd stepped off the plane at Phoenix Airport.

And then it kept going.

My insides started to go cold again. It wasn't panic this time. It was a slow, creeping dread.

There was stuff here from before I'd come to Phoenix. Way before.

School photos from back in Brisbane. Three-year-old printouts of an *About Me* website they'd made us all do at the start of Year 7. A newspaper clipping, curled and yellowing, from when my primary school debating team won the state competition. Progress reports from my preschool, held to the wall with old, rusting pins. A copy of my birth certificate.

They had just as much stuff on Luke. At least

twice as much on Peter.

Someone was watching us. And they had been for a very long time.

"Who do you think they are?" I asked, trying to mask the fear in my voice.

There was a thud from the next room, then a clattering sound, like something metal dropping to the floor.

I tore my eyes away from the timeline, spinning around to face the door in the corner of the room. I started creeping around the far side of the table – but then a sudden movement on one of the laptop screens caught my eye.

Footage from another security camera. But not one of Shackleton's. The image was grainy black-and-white, and it kept flickering, like it was being shot on a much older camera.

It was a picture of the bush. Judging by the angle, the camera must have been mounted somewhere up in one of the trees. A line of crumbling concrete ran through the shot – the remains of a wall. The camera was monitoring the entrance to this place.

And right now, it was also monitoring Calvin.

He was still there, pacing furiously back and forth across the tunnel entrance. He had his phone back out again. There was no sound coming from the computer, but from the look of his contorted face, he was screaming the ear off whoever was on the other end of that phone.

I kept walking. Nothing we could do about Calvin now.

I got to the door. Heard Luke scream from across the room.

And then my legs fell out from under me and I collapsed to the ground.

Chapter 30

The smashed fingers. The gash in my shoulder. The cuts and grazes from my fall into the grass.

All of them disappeared, swallowed up in the mind-crushing pain shattering out from the base of my spine. My eyes spun out of focus, screams exploding from my throat.

The suppressors still reached down here. And Calvin had finally gotten through to someone on his phone.

It was like needles tunneling through my legs. I looked down, and it seemed impossible that they weren't spewing blood or falling to pieces or engulfed in flames. All this agony and nothing to show for it.

Luke dragged himself across the ground towards me, clawing under the table, face red with the effort. He collapsed, moaning in pain.

I gathered my strength, trying to push myself up onto my feet. For a moment, the pain seemed to ebb away a bit and I threw myself forward, making a grab at the door handle in front of me.

Then another wave hit me and I fell, my head smacking against the door.

I knocked the handle on my way down.

The door swung open.

I crashed through to the next room, not even noticing the impact as my body hit the floor, pain receptors already pushed as far as they could go. I lay there, writhing in the doorway, clawing at the small of my back, trying pointlessly to make it stop.

And then, dimly through the pain, like it was coming from underwater ...

"Jordan!"

I pried open my eyes, fighting to hold still enough to take in the room.

Brighter light in here. Sinks and benches and metal instruments. Surgical stuff. Other equipment too.

More needles launched themselves down through my legs and I forgot about all of it, almost throwing up, almost blacking out.

I could hear Luke close behind me, grinding his teeth, still pulling towards the door.

"Jordan!" the voice screamed again. "Up here!"

I forced my eyes back into focus. I was lying at the foot of a bed like the ones in the other rooms. The floor was a mess. Cereal and milk everywhere. A metal bowl and spoon lay on the ground near my head.

I strained to look up, stretching to my hands and knees.

He was lying propped up on the bed. Blood soaking through the bandage around his head. Left jaw all cut and bruised. His hands were free, but everything else below his shoulders was strapped down to the mattress.

"PETER!"

His face was wracked with fear. "Jordan, no! Oh no. Get out! Get out of here before they –!"

Twin cries from Luke and me drowned out the rest of his warning. My knees collapsed sideways and I face-planted into the spilled cornflakes. I pushed up, slipped in the milk, and crumpled down again.

"Jordan, please," said Peter. "They're coming! You have to get out!"

A door flew open across the room, and a Eurasian man with spiky black hair ran in. He was dressed in a long, white lab coat that looked a bit too big for him.

White robes, I thought dimly.

The man stopped, almost treading on me. He wasn't even a man. He couldn't have been more than a few years older than me. He took one look at Luke and me, thrashing on the floor, and dashed across to the sink.

"Mum!" he yelled back over his shoulder. "They're here!"

He pumped some soap into his hand and ran the water, glancing back down at us with a mix of excitement and … something else.

A woman strode into the room. Probably in her mid-fifties. Graying hair, frameless glasses, and a matching lab coat. She had a pickaxe slung over her right shoulder.

The woman turned to the boy. "Everything ready?"

He nodded, rinsing the soap off his hands.

The woman propped her pickaxe up against the wall. She came straight past me and stared down at Luke, still only halfway through the door.

"Luke Hunter," she said, folding her arms. "At last. You have no idea how long we've waited for you to arrive."

The PHOENIX FILES

arrival

contact

mutation

underground

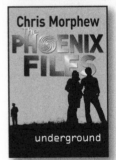

fallout

doomsday

Someone in Phoenix is plotting
to wipe out the human race.
And the clock is already ticking.
THERE ARE ONE HUNDRED DAYS
UNTIL THE END OF THE WORLD.

Born in Sydney, Australia, in 1985, Chris Morphew spent his childhood writing stories about dinosaurs and time machines. More recently he has written for the best-selling *Zac Power* series. *The Phoenix Files* is his first series for young adults.